REA
ALLEN COUNTY PUBLIC LIBRARY
S0-BXB-441

# MISSOURI MADAM

Spur froze in place at the edge of the kitchen and waited. When the seconds quieted again he moved to the living room off the kitchen. Spur found a fancy lady sleeping nude on a couch. On the floor below her lay a man equally clothesless. He stirred as Spur stepped on a squeaking floor board.

The man came up in two seconds, wide awake and a big .44 in his fist aimed at the noise. Spur shot him in the shoulders, slamming the gun out of his hand. The man screamed and Spur heard action all over the house....

NOV 1 1 2004
WESTERN

Also in the *Spur* Series:
**SPUR #1: ROCKY MOUNTAIN VAMP**
**SPUR #2: CATHOUSE KITTEN**
**SPUR #3: INDIAN MAID**
**SPUR #4: SAN FRANCISCO STRUMPET**
**SPUR #5: WYOMING WENCH**
**SPUR #6: TEXAS TART**
**SPUR #7: MONTANA MINX**
**SPUR #8: SANTA FE FLOOZY**
**SPUR #9: SALT LAKE LADY**
**SPUR #10: NEVADA HUSSY**
**SPUR #11: NEBRASKA NYMPH**
**SPUR #12: GOLD TRAIN TRAMP**
**SPUR #13: RED ROCK REDHEAD**
**SPUR #14: SAVAGE SISTERS**
**SPUR #15: HANG SPUR McCOY!**
**SPUR #16: RAWHIDER'S WOMAN**
**SPUR #18: MISSOURI MADAM**
**SPUR #19: HELENA HELLION**
**SPUR #20: COLORADO CUTIE**
**SPUR #21: TEXAS TEASE**
**SPUR #22: DAKOTA DOXY**
**SPUR #23: SAN DIEGO SIRENS**
**SPUR #24: DODGE CITY DOLL**
**SPUR #25: LARAMIE LOVERS**

SPUR #18

# MISSOURI MADAM

DIRK FLETCHER

LEISURE BOOKS NEW YORK CITY

A LEISURE BOOK®

November 2004

Published by

Dorchester Publishing Co., Inc.
200 Madison Avenue
New York, NY 10016

If you purchased this book without a cover you should be aware that this book is stolen property. It was reported as "unsold and destroyed" to the publisher and neither the author nor the publisher has received any payment for this "stripped book."

Copyright © 1986 by Dirk Fletcher

All rights reserved. No part of this book may be reproduced or transmitted in any form or by any electronic or mechanical means, including photocopying, recording or by any information storage and retrieval system, without the written permission of the publisher, except where permitted by law.

ISBN 0-8439-2409-8

The name "Leisure Books" and the stylized "L" with design are trademarks of Dorchester Publishing Co., Inc.

Printed in the United States of America.

Visit us on the web at www.dorchesterpub.com.

SPUR #18

# MISSOURI MADAM

# 1

Sam Bass watched from well down the dusty street as his four men wandered one at a time into the train station at Short Falls. The station was brand new on this just opened feeder line of the Missouri & Texas Central railroad that angled on into Springfield, Missouri in the southwest corner of the state.

Sam heard the whistle of the afternoon express and grinned as he led his horse down the street toward the station. usually the M & T never stopped at Short Falls, but it would today. The red signal would be out and the steam engine would drag the cars to a halt. Sam loosened the .44 in his holster and eyed the sawed off shotgun in his saddle boot.

Everything was ready out here.

Inside the station Wyatt Turner had locked both doors, ordered the three waiting passengers to lie on the floor, and watched as Louis slapped around the station manager until he admitted that he could stop the express, and pulled a lever that would lift the red flag.

Wyatt went to the telegraph key and ripped the

sending instrument off the wires and pushed it inside his shirt. They might not have another one.

The two trainmen now lay on the floor in a closet, bound and locked inside. Wyatt and Louis ambled out on the platform which was built up to meet the height of the train car boxes for ease in unloading freight. A short time later Joe came out of the station, moved to his assigned spot and tried to look bored.

Hans, the last man out of the rail building had taken time to order the lone woman passenger to stand. He then thrust his hands inside the top of her dress and rubbed her breasts until she screamed and kicked him in the shins. He grinned and hurried outside.

The slow moving train came to a stop at the station platform at the same time Sam Bass walked up after tying his horse to the rail. Wyatt at the head of the platform jumped in the engine doorway and leveled his six-gun at the engineer and fireman.

"Move the train or die in your shoes!" Louis hissed. "Get us two miles out of town and then stop. Now, asshole!"

The engineer nodded and pushed the levers. Steam whistled out of the cylinders as the big drive wheels began to spin on the steel rails, then caught hold and the eight car train moved forward gradually, then slowly picked up speed.

The other four members of the Sam Bass gang had stepped on board the train without incident. When the train was moving fast enough to discourage anyone from jumping off, Louis went into the first passenger car.

"Nobody move or you're dead!" Louis shouted. "Gents get out your wallets and purses, ladies all your jewelry and 'course any gold watches." Louis grabbed a hat off a man in the first seat and held it out.

"Just fill up the hat and nobody is gonna get hurt." To emphasize his point, Louis blasted a .44 round through the nearby window. The noise of the pistol in the confined space was much louder than usual. One woman screamed.

"Shut up!" Louis yelled. "Now get out the cash and jewelry. Don't want to have to yank no necklaces off or anything like that." The people knew not to object or try to stop him. After all, this was the year 1878, and train robbers were the talk of the nation.

At the far end of the car Hans lifted his six-gun and added his comments.

"Just don't get frisky, anybody, cause I'm right here with my trusty .44 looking right down your nose. Now get out those wallets!"

One gang in Texas robbed trains five times near Dallas in fifty days. Everyone knew train robbers were desperados, as quick to kill a person as they were to make conversation.

Sam Bass and Joe had moved through the second passenger car directly to the express car where the mail and valuables were carried and where the safe was located.

The two men in the express car had no warning that anything was out of the ordinary. They often stopped at red flag stations to take on mail or pouches and were moving again at once.

The express door was locked as usual. Sam Bass put three .44 slugs into the locking mechanism. At once Joe drove his shoulder and all two hundred pounds of his weight into the partition and it sprang open.

Sam Bass shot again into the roof of the car, just

to stop any gunplay by the expressmen. One was a small clerk, the other was the one Sam wanted.

"No wasted time, gents, open the safe," Sam bellowed. Neither man moved. Sam picked one of them and lifted his .44. He had one round left in it. "You, open the safe or I'll blow your brains all over the car," Sam thundered.

"Please no! I'm the mail clerk," the man Sam aimed at yelped. "I don't even know where the safe is!" The man dropped to his knees. Sam pushed him to one side and swung his pistol toward the second man. Sweat beaded on his upper lip.

"Glad to open the safe, mister, but I don't know the combination. They changed it just before we left St. Louis and wouldn't tell me. Don't get opened until we hit Dallas."

Sam moved the muzzle and shot the man in the right shoulder. The expressman slammed back against the mail sacks and then caught his balance. He held his left hand over the wound, agony painted his face.

"Killing me won't help. I don't know the damn numbers!"

Sam had learned to recognize when a man was telling the truth. He motioned Joe up and took four sticks of the new fangled dynamite out of a sack, fixed it with sticky tape and wrapped more tape around the handle of the safe.

"Move these civilians out to the vestibule," Sam snapped at Joe who herded the two workers to the far end of the car and out the door to the narrow platform between cars.

Sam lit the fuse and went out the other door.

Thirty seconds later, the safe blew. The explosion blasted the sliding side door on the express car half off its track, blew a hundred pieces of mail around the car, but ruined the locking mechanism on the safe and jolted the heavy door completely off one hinge.

When he heard the blast in the engine ahead, Wyatt ordered the engineer to stop the train. Then he tied up both men, dropped down from the engine and walked back to the express car along the cinder filled right of way.

Sam sat on the floor in front of the safe grinning. There was a wooden box sealed with wax that held five hundred freshly minted gold double eagles; ten thousand dollars!

Sam pawed through the rest of the goods, found some stocks and bonds that he didn't understand and left them. He grabbed a sack of silver coins and a packet of what looked like grant deeds. He took the thirty-five pound box of gold coins to the edge of the side door.

The train had stopped. He couldn't budge the sliding door, so went out the one he had come in. Sam dropped to the right of way on the right hand side of the train facing the engine. He saw his four men ready to leave the train.

Down the tracks a quarter of a mile he could see a small trail of dust. That would be Charlie bringing up the horses. Quickly he called his men and then hurried into the brush at the side of the tracks, and only then did they hear two pistols firing at them from the train.

"Somebody is damn brave now!" Louis said. He held up a hat filled with greenbacks and gold and silver coins. "Must have over five hundred dollars in here, Sam! Then we got two gold watches and some rings and things."

"Good," Sam said. "Every little bit counts." Sam was well aware of the value of a dollar. The average cowboy worked for $25 a month and food. A clerk in a store might make $30 a month. They worked all year for $360!

Sam had thought of breaking open the box of gold coins and spreading around the weight, but he decided to keep the box himself. They got to the dirt road that ran a hundred yards from the train tracks and waited. The train still sat where it had been. Nobody had untied the engineer yet.

Three minutes later Charlie rode up with his string of horses and each man grabbed his own and mounted up.

"Which way?" Wyatt called.

"South," Sam said. "Heading for Texas. This is too damn far north to suit me. Nice little valley over there that runs down into the Ozarks. You boys ever been in the Ozark Mountains?"

The heads shook.

"How'd we do, Sam?" Louis called.

"Did a mite bit good, boys. Safe had a box of brand new double gold eagles . . . ten thousand dollars worth!"

Everyone whooped in total joy. Most of them had never seen that much money in their lives.

"That's two thousand for each of us!" Joe bellowed.

Sam grinned and waved them forward like he was in the army horse soldiers. "Let's ride, boys. We'll split it up later."

They rode for three hours and on the gradual up slope they could watch behind them and see that there was no pursuit. Sam knew exactly why. Planning. Good plans produce good results. He had worked on the best methods of robbing trains until he had it down to an exact science.

He took over the station well in advance of the

train's arrival. He ripped out the telegraph key so it would take time to notify anyone of the robbery. Then he had moved the train two miles out of town so no one in town could oppose the robbery. Finally he had placed his men in precise positions with specific jobs to do. His get away was also orchestrated.

Sam could not remember how many trains he and his changing band had robbed. Dozens by now. His first robbery was not so successful. Sam chuckled to himself remembering it.

That first outing had been on March 25, 1877, when he and two friends decided to rob a stagecoach not far out of Deadwood in Dakota territory. They would steal everything of value from the strong box and the passengers.

Frank Towle and Little Reddy McKimmie were the other two members of his gang. They got to the stage, challenged it and told the driver to stop, but Frank didn't get his job done of stopping the horses. He fired a shot, which spooked the horses and they took off charging down the rough stage road.

McKimmie tried to help and lifted his shotgun and fired. The buckshot killed the driver, Johnny Slaughter, who tumbled off the high perch and the reins went slack.

That was all the horses needed and they went wild "running away" with no one to control them. They charged down the roadway, smart enough to stay on the comparatively level area and raced themselves into a lather. Eventually an adventurous passenger caught the reins and pulled the horses to a stop.

The runaway horses had dragged along with them a strongbox with $15,000 inside, which Sam Bass never saw. He kicked McKimmie out of the gang and brought in more men and tried again.

On his very first train robbery he did better. But this job was planned down to the last eyelash. They took on the Union Pacific train in Nebraska near the town of Ogallala. Joel Collins had taken over as head of the gang, and they decided to hit the #4 Express when it paused at the water tank at 10:48, September 17, 1877.

A half hour before train time they took over the small station, tore out the telegraph key, and forced the agent to put out a red light so the express would stop.

It worked to perfection and was a haul that netted them $60,000 in new double eagle gold coins. They tried to get into the safe, but couldn't passing up another $200,000. It was the biggest money robbery that Sam Bass ever participated in. He always kept trying to equal it.

Sam held up his hand now as they topped a small rise along a chattering stream. They had been working up a series of valleys and were nearing the foothills to the Ozarks and their forested slopes ahead.

It was close to dark, when Sam spotted a small rancher's cabin next to the creek.

He talked to his men for a moment, then they vanished into some brush and he rode up to the door and called out.

"Hello. The house? Anyone there?"

A shotgun poked through the open door.

"Yeah? What you want?" a gruff voice asked.

"Mean you no harm. Stranger in these parts and I guess I got lost. I was heading for Branson. This the right way?"

The door came open another few inches, and Sam could see a whiskered face behind the double barrels of the scatter gun.

"Yep, it's the way, but you got a long piece to go yet. Riding alone?"

"My Injun squaw didn't want to come," Sam said grinning.

"Hail, you sound right enough. Want to lite and have a bite of supper? We just about to sit down."

"Appreciate it. My name is Sam."

He went to the door and inside the rough log cabin. The man with the shotgun also had a sidearm. Hovering over the stove was a girl of maybe eighteen, who was dishing up stew from a big copper pot. She was tall, a little plump with large breasts straining against the gingham dress top.

"Name's Hawkins," the man said. "Daughter is Hattie."

"Evening, Hawkins, Miss. I'm Sam. That stew smells mighty good."

"Sit and eat," Hattie said evenly. When her father looked away, she grinned at him, her eyes dancing.

Hawkins put down the shotgun and they ate, then when Hattie was clearing away the dishes, Sam lifted his six-gun and trained it on the man.

"Sorry, folks, but I do have some friends who would also like a bite to eat."

Hawkins growled and started to move his hand toward his pistol, but a round from Sam's revolver dug into the wooden table and slanted off into the wall.

"Easy like, Hawkins. Hand me your iron, butt first." The owner of the cabin did, his face angry.

"Come in boys!" Sam called. The other five men trooped into the room, tied Hawkins hand and foot and rolled him on the bunk. Hattie fed the rest of them, then smiled again at Sam.

"Sam, I'm getting me somewhat sleepy. Don't care where the rest of the men sleep, but I got me a bed back here, if'n you be even so little interested."

Sam was not the biggest man in the group. He stood five feet, eight inches tall and weighed one hundred, forty pounds. He had a well groomed handlebar moustache and a full head of dark hair which he parted just off center on the left side.

Sam caught Hattie's hand and led her into the end of the cabin where a blanket walled off one part of the small cabin. She grabbed his hands at once and pushed them up to her full breasts.

"Sam, it ain't often that I see a good looking young man like you! I just can't wait to get you all over and inside me!"

Sam undressed her slowly, played with her breasts until she soared into two climaxes, then stripped her and took off his clothes. He pushed her down on the bed and straddled her. Before he knew it she had grabbed his stiff rod and pulled it up so she could take it in her mouth.

A few minutes later Hattie moved him back down on her hot and ready body and admitted it had been almost a year since she'd had a man in he bed. She made up for it with Sam. By morning he figured he had slept only about a half hour, and he was so exhausted that he couldn't get it up any more.

Hattie pulled his soft pud into her mouth but it was no use, Sam was played out. Hattie took his hand and pushed it between her legs and stuffed three fingers inside her.

"Once more with your fingers, darling Sam, then I'll get breakfast." She kissed him. "Sweet fucker Sam, you send your boys on ahead and you stay on a few days. I'll take care of my old man. I get better the more fucking I do. In about three days I'll really show you a wild time!"

Sam dressed, had breakfast, and told Hattie not

to untie her paw until they were out of sight. He really did have to leave. Hattie swore at Sam, ran for the shot gun and they barely got it away from her before she blasted it at Sam.

Her dress top came open and her big breasts swung out in the struggle, but Wyatt got the shotgun. Wyatt was mad at Sam for a week because Sam made them ride out right then, without giving Wyatt his turn to crawl over the eager farmer's daughter.

Sam Bass had learned that robbing trains and making love to strange women did not mix. One or the other, but almost never both on the same outing. He had made an exception for Hattie, and didn't recover for two days until they were in Branson. By then it was time to take a rest, watch the back trail, and give the men free rein on the two fancy ladies in the small town's only saloon. Sam decided to rest up a few more days.

# 2

Spur McCoy settled down in the soft seat of the railraod passenger car and looked out the window at the Missouri landscape slashing by at thirty miles an hour. Amazing how quickly these Iron Horses could cover the ground. Coast to coast in seven days if you made the right train connections!

Why, he remembered when . . . Spur tilted his hat down over his eyes and grinned. He was sounding like an old timer, not a young buck ready to take on the world. Spur was not about to challenge the whole place, he had his hands full right now tracking down Sam Bass, train bandit.

Sam Bass had robbed his first stage coach last year, and now in the spring of 1878 he had more than a dozen train heists on his criminal record. He had come to the attention of the United States Secret Service when he robbed five trains near Dallas, Texas within a six week period.

Spur's boss, General Wilton D. Halleck in Washington, D.C. had telegraphed Spur in Denver to get on Sam Bass's trail and to ride him into jail or a grave, either one was fine with Gen. Halleck. The service had been getting pressure from all over Washington evidently.

Spur McCoy was a U.S. Secret Service Agent, and while few in number they were starting to make a name for themselves in the law enforcement field. Just after the Civil War, the Secret Service was literally the only law agency that could cross state lines. The service had been started by Congress with the specific job of protecting the U.S. currency against counterfeiters. Their assignments quickly broadened to almost any interstate or interterritorial crime of dispute.

Spur had joined the Service as soon as it was founded. He had served for two years in the war as an infantry officer winding up as a captain. Then he was called to Washington, D.C. to serve as aide to Senator Arthur B. Walton, a long time family friend and the senior senator from the state of New York.

Spur took the assignment, then went with the Secret Service. After serving six months in Washington D.C., Spur found himself shipped to St. Louis, Missouri where he would head up the Service's activities in the states west of there.

He was assigned the position because he was the best horseman in the Service and had recently won the pistol competition. General Halleck assumed he would need both skills covering the West. The general had been right.

Spur was better educated than most western lawmen. He grew up in New York City where his father was a wealthy store owner and importer. Spur went to Harvard and graduated with a specialty in history. Then he worked for his father for two years.

The train jolted and Spur's hat fell to the floor. Before he could retrieve it a sparkling young woman bent and grabbed it and handed it to him. She had come and sat opposite him while he had been daydreaming under his hat. He smiled at her, thanked her and she smiled then looked away.

"Thank you again, Miss. That was most courteous of you," Spur said.

She glanced at him, aloof and poised. Then she grinned and dimples punctured her cheeks. "Welcome," she said softly and Spur wanted to get to know her better, but she stood as the train stopped and walked to the end of the car and got off at some small Missouri town.

A tall farmer met her outside the train and kissed her possessively. Spur lifted his brows and went back to his thoughts.

Sam Bass. The man liked to travel. From Deadwood up in the Dakota Territories, to Ogallala in Nebraska, then down to Dallas. Spur had been on his way to St. Louis to head south when he got the new telegram.

SPUR MCCOY. DENVER. SAM BASS ROBBED TRAIN OUTSIDE OF SPRINGFIELD, MISSOURI TODAY. ON THE MISSOURI & TEXAS CENTRAL LINE. PROCEED WITH ALL SPEED TO AREA, AND TRACK DOWN CULPRIT. THIS MISSION TAKES PRIORITY OVER ANY OTHER. SIGNED, HALLECK, SALES MANAGER.

The day before, the train mail had brought him a dozen pages of facts and pictures of Sam Bass. Sam was well known in the press, even posing for pictures with his gang. He was only twenty six years old, but was a master at robbing trains. Spur hoped this would be Sam's last train job.

Spur dug the papers out and went over them again. Sam had been born July 21, 1851 on a farm outside of Mitchell, Indiana. He was one of ten children. Both his mother and father were dead by the time he was thirteen and he was on his own. When he was nineteen he went to Texas to become a cowboy. He got a job on a farm and a year later moved to Denton, Texas where he worked as a stablehand.

He developed a taste for whiskey, and gambling, especially at the small race track in Denton where horses ran every Sunday. Near the end of 1875 Sam was run out of Denton by a posse after he was mixed up in a beating after an argument.

He drifted to San Antonio and in the summer of 1876 with two partners drove seven hundred head of beef to Kansas and the railroad. From there they worked up to Deadwood where they tried to pull a stage coach robbery that went sour.

Then Sam was in on the Big Springs, Nebraska robbery of the train that netted more than $60,000. After that he started his own gang.

Spur pushed aside the papers and stared out the window again. They would be in Springfield in two hours. That meant he was over two days behind the robbers. A mighty cold trail. But at least he had some kind of a trail. Which direction would they move out of the Springfield area?

Spur checked a map spread out over his knees. He guessed they would head south, back to his homeland. That direction led into one of the least populated sections of Missouri and into the Ozark Mountains. Spur had heard some wild tales about the Ozarks, how there was almost no law in some of the counties. That would be an attraction for Sam Bass.

When Spur got to the station he would see what the railroad people knew. Some of them could be most helpful. One of the trainmen must have seen which direction they took when they left the train. It was a hope.

Spur pushed the hat down over his eyes and leaned back on the soft cushion. He was going to be on the trail again soon enough, and sleeping on the ground, waking up stiff and sore. Maybe he should get a nice cushy job as a town marshall somewhere and settle down. Naw!

The jolting of the trail as the cars banged together when the train braked to a stop at Short Falls, eighteen miles east of Springfield, stirred Spur again. This was the site of the robbery.

Spur McCoy grabbed his carpetbag and slid down the steps to the ground and walked across to the small depot. There was no one there to meet him. A quick inquiry showed that none of the train people were on hand who had been on the robbed train two days before. Spur pushed back his low-crowned brown Stetson and scowled at the telegraph operator.

"I'm a federal lawman come here to try and find Sam Bass. Is there anyone who can tell me which direction the gang rode off after the robbery?"

"Fer cats' sakes, course there is, young feller," the key man said staring at Spur from watery blue eyes.

"Good, who is it?"

"Me. I talked to all of them when they backed the train into the station."

"So, kind sir. Which way did Sam Bass ride?"

"South, straight into the Ozarks." He wiped his eyes with a red trainman's handkerchief half as big as he was. "Just damn glad I don't got to go into them Ozarks. Hear tell lots of folks ride in there . . . then they just ain't never heard of again."

"And you'll swear that's the way Sam and his gang rode? How long did these eyewitnesses of yours see them heading that way?"

"Long as they could spot them from top of the train. That string of cars was 'bout two miles out, more or less. Old Clint, he's the engineer on that run, he figured he better back her in and tell us what happened. The brakeman, Arch, he stood on top a box car and watched Sam and his bunch till they went behind a line of trees. Heading south all the way, they was."

Spur handed him a telegram message and a greenback dollar bill. "Send this out right away, if it's no trouble. I'd appreciate it."

The telegrapher became all business again, lowered his green eyeshade over the watery blue eyes and read it out loud.

"Just so I get it right, you know. Says: To General Halleck, Washington D.C. Arrived on robbery site. In pursuit. Signed McCoy. Yep, I can send that."

"Much obliged," Spur said. "Oh, is there a livery stable in town?"

"Nope. But we got a blacksmith who's got an extra horse or two. Down half a block, two houses from the tracks."

Spur thanked him and went to find a horse. He hoped the old nag he probably would find would make it into the Ozarks.

McCoy had ridden a full day now toward the forested ridges ahead of him. He covered about twenty five miles the first day along the thin track of a stagecoach road that was used once a week to haul goods, mail and passengers into Branson.

From what he could find out from the locals, Branson would be the best spot for Sam Bass and his gang to stop and rest a day or so and perhaps kick up their heels a bit before they rode on south—

if that was the direction they headed.

With no other choice, Spur angled along the coach road. An hour before sunset he saw a smoke to the left and rode up a small rise off the trail to investigate. A little ranch showed below, two pole corrals, a small barn, and a log house made from local material. Maybe two hundred head of steers and cows and calves in open range below the house. Maybe he could get a meal and an inside place to sleep for the night.

He rode up and saw pansys and hollyhocks blooming outside the front door. There was a woman here, that was for certain.

"Hello!" Spur called loudly.

A shotgun angled through the front door.

"Yeah, what do you want?" a woman's voice asked.

"Passing through, wondered if I could rent a room or buy some supper? I'm short on supplies."

"You alone? My husband wants to know. You alone?"

"Fact is, I am, ma'am. Heading for Branson. This the way?"

"This is the way." The door swung open and she lowered the shotgun. "Lite and tie your horse. I can find some supper for you if'n you not too picky."

As Spur swung down, he saw she was blonde, hair around her shoulders, younger than the voice indicated, maybe twenty-five or six. She brushed hair out of her gray eyes as he tied his horse. One hand rested on her hip and the other hung at her side.

"Come far?"

"Railroad at Short Falls."

"Anything happening there?" she asked. He saw that her eyes really were pale gray, and her skin was soft and only slightly tanned. She did not spend a lot of time outdoors.

"Sam Bass robbed the train," Spur said.

"Sam Bass, that Texas badman? What's he doing way up here?"

"Looking for more trains, I reckon."

She laughed and he saw the bodice of her dress strain as her breasts thrust forward.

"Come in, come in. We don't get company often up here." She went ahead of him into the one room cabin. It was as neat as a widow's Park Avenue apartment and just as fussy. She had not left her culture or her sense of neatness behind when she moved to this edge of the wilderness.

"My name is Ruth. What's yours?"

"Spur McCoy."

She held out her hand and shook his. "Pleased to meet you, Mr. McCoy."

"I'm pleased to meet you, and to find your ranch just when I needed it. This is a very nice room," Spur said. "Are you from New York?"

She looked up quickly, surprise on her face. She smiled, nodded and went to the wood burning kitchen range.

"I best be heating up some food for you. I don't eat much." She watched him from the stove. "Sit and rest yourself. Wash up out at the pump, you have a mind to." She turned now and he saw that she was slender, yet shapely. "How did you know I was from New York?"

"Just a guess, and the way you have this cabin furnished and how you keep it so neat. Reminds me of an aunt of mine in New York City, Brooklyn really."

"Good Lord, I'm from Brooklyn!" Her face was alive, remembering. Then she turned. "Better get the fire going."

"Let me," Spur said. She stepped back. He put in kindling, then larger wood, and pushed in a pitch stick under the kindling. He lit the turpentine-like pitch which ignited the rest of the wood.

"You've done that before," she said.

Spur saw no signs that a man lived in the cabin, no pipe, no boots, no horsewhip or square of chewing tobacco.

"Husband be gone long?"

She turned and watched him a minute. "For eternity. One of our bulls killed him six months ago. Been trying to make do with all the work around here with my two black hands. So far, so good."

She fixed a meal then. First she fried a thick beef-steak, then warmed up boiled potatoes, beets, carrots and peas that must have come from her garden, and then set out two big slabs of apple pie. He ate it all and drank three cups of coffee.

"Best apple pie I ever had," Spur said.

"Cinnamon. I use just the right amount of cinnamon and it perks up the flavor. Crust always was easy for me."

"The lonesome part must not be."

"True. Will you stay the night?"

"I can sleep on the floor."

"No reason. Bed's big enough for two, used to be, reckon it still is."

She soon finished the dishes and moved to the small couch where Spur sat smoking a thin black cheroot.

"Haven't smelled tobacco in this house for six months. Never liked it much before. Now, seems kind of nice."

She sat beside Spur, trimmed the coal oil lamp's wick a bit to lower the light, then turned to Spur.

"I won't beat around the bush, Spur. I am lonesome. No man's had his hands on me for six months, and I'm more than ready to share my bed with you. You a mind to?"

"Why don't we just see what happens, Ruthie." He bent forward and she moved toward him. He kissed her lips gently, then again. She moved closer and her arms went around him. Her mouth opened and Spur let her tongue dart into his mouth.

Ruthie groaned softly and held the kiss. She made animal sounds in her throat and gently leaned backward, pulling him down on top of her. The kiss ended and she looked at him.

"Oh, lordy, but it has been a long time! I'd forgotten how it always gets me so warm. Lordy!"

She reached up to be kissed again and he moved so he lay half on her and half off. He kissed her, then lifted his hand to one of her breasts.

"Yes, yes!" she said through the kiss. His hand wormed between them through the buttons on the print dress top and closed around her breast.

"Yes, sweetheart! Yes! play with them. They are all yours. Do anything you want to, sweetheart!" Her eyes were closed and Spur guessed she was pretending her husband was feeling her again.

She let him lift the dress up and over her hips, then take it off over her head. Under it she had on only a thin chemise and no drawers or underwear.

"No need," she said in explanation. "No one to impress, no one to entice." She slipped off the chemise and her breasts were hand sized, delicately nippled with small brown areolas.

"Yes, I'm not a virgin. We lost our baby after six months, sweet little girl child. She had been sickly from the start." Ruth shook her head. "I don't want to think about the ones who are gone. I want to feel of the one who is here."

Carefully, slowly she undressed him. "I haven't done this in so long!" she said again and again. "I love to undress a man. It gets me all worked up."

Spur lay on the bed and pull on top of him. She lowered one breast into his waiting mouth and laughed.

"Yes! A woman does love that! Makes us glad we're different, and we have tits men love to chew and suck on. No milk now, but there was a time." She blinked back tears, then changed putting her other breast down for him to lick.

Then her hips began grinding against him.

"I can't wait!" she yowled. "Do me right now, quick before the fire goes out. Right not!"

She rolled over and spread her legs, and pulled Spur with her. He lowered and thrust and she swallowed him in one stroke her inner muscles closing around him like a lasso in a crazy way, gripping and releasing.

"Do me now!" she said again and thrust her hips up to meet him. "Faster!"

"You do like it, don't you, Ruth?"

"Yes! Yes! Who says a woman can't like sex as much as a man? This woman does love to get fucked."

The word made her climax and she screamed and wailed, her hips pounding him higher and higher until the spasms shook her, dropping her back to the bed, rattling her like a morning express with empty boxcars.

She scratched Spur's back with her fingernails, shouted again and then bit him on the shoulder. Gradually the spasms faded and she lay limp for a minute staring up at him from the pale gray eyes.

"Glorious! There is nothing half so good! Marvelous! No wonder women let men walk all over them . . . it's all so we can get fucked!

"Heavens! I forgot about you. You didn't make it while I did I don't guess. But then I'd never feel you." She ground her hips a moment under him. "Lordy, but he's still stiff as a telegraph pole." She humped her hips and worked her inner muscles and at once Spur felt a jolt as the freight began to move down the long tube to freedom.

He pumped and groaned and pounded the bed beside her and when he at last climaxed he drove her halfway to the floor through the feather bed and the straw mattress over the springs. She was laughing and crying when he at last shot his final load and collapsed on her.

"Lordy, I never thought you would ever get done. You are some long staying man. I like it that way. No, don't move." She put her arms around his back, pinning them together.

"I like to lay this way for a while, do you mind?"

"No."

"Go to sleep if you want to, I don't mind."

"Not feeling sleepy yet. I say once is never enough."

"Oh good! When I saw you I figured at least four times, maybe five. What do you think?"

Spur laughed softly. "You do love it, don't you? When I get past four I do start to think about sleeping."

"Well, cowboy, we'll have to test you out and try for a new record, your own personal best. I'd say you're around six."

Spur laughed again and kissed her. "I see this is going to be a long night, with not a whole lot of sleep involved."

"Damn right," Ruth said quickly. "I get a big stallion like you in my corral, I'm not gonna let you go with just one or two shots. I got to come out even on all the apple pie you ate somehow." They both laughed.

About midnight they got out of bed and renewed their energy with fresh boiled coffee and more apple pie. Spur had two more pieces and a slab of home-made cheddar cheese. It was a pale yellow and aged only six months, but tangy and good.

He watched her walking around the small cabin as naked as the day she was birthed and not a bit self conscious about it.

"What are your plans, Ruth? You figure to stay here and prove up on your homestead?"

"Plan to. Take me another year and a half. If my two hands will stay on for grub and tobacco and a couple of dollars a month, I might make it. They was slaves in Mississippi before the war. Now they say there are just happy to have a place to live and to be treated halfway like free men." She watched him.

"Man, you are naked, you know that?"

Spur sipped the scalding coffee. "Wondered why I was getting chilly. You think of anything we could do to get warmed up again?"

"I'll ponder on it." She stared at him. "Spur, never did tell me what you do. You know something about ranches, I'd wager. Want to stay on here? We get on great in bed, and you can help run the place. Half of it's yours. No preacher, nothing. Just living together and working the place. Taking it as it comes. Kids is okay with me. Whatever. I like you, Spur."

"And you're not going back to Brooklyn?"

"All that coal dust and grime and all those people? Not a chance in a million. I like the wide open country. Besides, my pa kicked me out of the house. I got more here than I would have back there. How about it, partners in the ranch and in ownership and use of the double bed?"

"Let's talk about that in the morning. We're only half way to six. I used to know a little black girl down in New Orleans who had the wildest way to make love. Want to try it?"

"How wild, Spur?"

"Not anything hurtful, you game?"

Ruth was.

The next morning, she fried him eggs, used the last of a slab of bacon from the cool house in the well, and cooked up more hash brown potatoes than he could eat.

"You thinking of my proposition?" Ruth asked.

"Some."

"So?"

"Got me a job to do, first. Sam Bass. Badass Sam Bass, got to go find him. Afraid I wouldn't be much good as a rancher or a farmer. Like to keep moving."

"Back to some of that New Orleans black cunt, right?" Ruth said. She shrugged. "Never hoped in a year and a half that I could make you stay. A woman has some ways to persuade a man, but you done seen all of mine by now. One for the road?"

"A kiss is 'bout all the strength I have left, you sexy lady. Seven, wasn't it?"

Ruth grinned. "At least I'll have that as a new record." She turned and wiped her eyes, then looked back. "Now get your pretty ass out of here before I start blubbering!"

Spur waved and rode out south back to the road that wound higher into the foothills toward Branson.

# 3

McCoy never looked back at the woman as he rode away. Yes, it would be something of a relief to swing down, kiss her and help her run her ranch, their ranch, she had said. But Spur McCoy just wasn't quite ready to do that yet. He told her he had to keep moving, to see what was over the next hill.

To find out where Sam Bass was and how he could help bring him to justice and remove a threat to the rail transport of the nation. He moved the nag out at the pace he thought she could hold up under for four hours. Then he would give her a rest, lay in the sun for a half hour and be moving again.

A full, hard day of riding brought Spur McCoy to the edge of the quiet little Ozark mountain village of Branson, population 312, elevation 1,237 feet. Spur didn't like the feel of the place as he sat his horse a quarter of a mile away. There was something about it he didn't understand. He made a small camp in a patch of woodsy brush a half mile from town.

The secret agent left his horse and rifle at his hidden camp and with his .45 Colt on his thigh, walked into town for a beer and to see what he could learn. The town wasn't much. One dirt street with a block's worth of stores and four or five avenues winding off that were filled with small houses built of clapboard and cedar shingles.

He saw a one room school and a small church. Spur counted four saloons, two small general stores and a half a dozen other shops and businesses along the lightly built "commercial" block. Branson was the county seat of Taney county, but he couldn't locate any kind of courthouse.

By then it was nearly dark. The second bar seemed to be the most popular, Cat's Claw, the sign said so he pushed through the bat wing doors. It was mid rustic, even for the mountains. The bar was of varnished quarter cut shortleaf pine and white oak alternated. The bar rail near the floor was an oak two by four well worn down by boots. Along the far wall stood a row of poker tables and a few more small tables for serious drinkers. Six kerosene lamps lit the room in a kind of murky light so the card players had to squint to be sure of their hands.

Spur bought a beer for a nickel and stood at the bar making rings on the polished surface with the cold glass. Plenty of ice in the underground ice house must be available in Branson. They probably had a winter freeze ice pond. Within a half hour he heard that there was a group of six strangers in town. They had moved into the old Parsons house and appeared to be staying for a time.

"Don't know who'n hell they are," the barkeep told a friend. He polished a beer mug and waggled his head. "But they got money, new looking gold double eagles. Brand new ones. The ridges on the edges ain't ever been worn off. Now where would a bunch of shiftless looking hombres like them get just minted double eagles?"

"Does make a feller wonder, don't it?" the man at the bar said, laughed softly and tilted his mug of beer.

At the next saloon, which was less crowded and where a beer cost a dime, Spur asked a stranger where the Parsons place was.

"You got to be new in town to ask that question," the man said. He held out his hand. "I'm Jones, run the general store. You need anything, I probably got it."

Spur shook his hand. "McCoy, just passing through. Trying to locate a friend."

"Parsons place is three houses beyond the school. It's the one with the faded white picket fence around it. Old man Parsons died about a year ago. Nobody knows who owns the place now. Evidently he had kin in Boston, but we don't know much about them. Nobody been keeping the place up much, but somebody rents it out now and then. Banker most likely."

Spur bought Jones a beer and they talked some more.

"I'm looking for some really good range breeding stock. Any around here?"

Jones just shook his head.

"For good breeding stock, you better stick to Texas, or Kansas. Most of the cattle in these parts are hodgepodge bastards, so mixed up they aren't any one breed at all. Mostly sold to locals for beef. Now and then there's a drive down grade to Springfield. Not much of good as cattle country around Branson. Now you move on down toward Springfield, you can find some better stock."

Spur left a while later, walked by the Parsons place and saw lights on in every window but one. He heard somebody singing a drunken, bawdy song and then the wild laugh of a female. It sounded like Sam and his boys were whooping it up. With ten thousand dollars worth of double gold eagles they could buy anything they wanted in town. And maybe anybody.

Spur hoped the whiskey was flowing well for the Sam Bass robber gang. That would make his work much easier. He would get some sleep and surprise the bunch about four A.M. when they were still drunk and too hungover to shoot straight.

McCoy walked back to his camp, slept, and woke up precisely at four A.M. He took his Henry with a full load of twelve rounds, his trusty Colt .45 in his holster and a second six-gun, a smaller, .32 caliber, for back up.

He walked into town and then circled around the house. Everything was quiet. The lights were all out. Spur tried the back door and found it unlocked. Quietly he eased inside and at once found a man sleeping in his own vomit on the kitchen floor, a whiskey bottle was still clutched in his right fist but it had all drained out on his pants.

Spur eased a hogsleg out of leather on the man's thigh, then tied his hands in front of him. The drunken robber stirred, said something in his sleep and laughed softly, then quieted. Spur used another length of heavy cord and tied the man's ankles together.

Spur heard someone roll out of bed overhead and hit the floor. There was drunken swearing, then the squeak of bedsprings, and a woman's giggle. Spur froze in place at the edge of the kitchen and waited. When the sounds quieted again he moved to the living room off the kitchen. Spur found a fancy lady sleeping nude on a couch. On the floor below her lay a man equally clothesless. He stirred as Spur stepped on a squeaking floor board.

The man came up in two seconds, wide awake and a big .44 in his fist aimed at the noise. Spur shot him in the shoulder, slamming the gun out of his hand. He screamed and Spur heard action all over the house.

The man lay bleeding against the sofa, where the fancy lady had sat up and grinned at Spur. "You like my big tits," she asked in a kind of automatic response to a frightening situation. She trembled, then fell on the couch.

Four shots blasted through the living room from a hallway. Spur heard windows open, another one break. He was flat on his belly behind a big bookcase and writing desk. Evidently Mr. Parsons had left the place completely furnished.

Another pair of slugs came through the door, then footsteps sounded down the hall and a door slammed.

Spur ran to the front window. He saw four half dressed men running down the street, looking back, swearing and waving their guns. Quickly Spur got the wounded man on his feet and pushed him into the kitchen.

The outlaw had just come out of his daze and tried to sit up. Spur cut loose his feet and helped him up.

"Either one of you jaspers want to say alive, you do damn quick what I tell you, savvy?"

Both men nodded.

"We're going out the back door and down the alley, turn the other way and find the sheriff's office. Understand?"

"Fer all the good it'll do you," the wounded man said. "First I need a doctor."

"No doctor. Slug went all the way through your

shoulder and your arm isn't broken. Only way you'll need a doctor is if you're half dead. Now move it."

They used up a half hour walking cautiously along the dark streets, down an alley and then around the front of the small building that had a poorly lettered sign that said "Sheriff's Office." The outside door was locked.

One of the men Spur had pushed ahead now laughed. Spur shot him an angry look and pounded on the wooden panel again.

"Yeah! yeah! Coming," a voice bellowed from inside at last. Another two or three minutes later the lock clicked, a bar was removed and the door swung open.

Sheriff Lund Parcheck peered out the door over a Remington .44 New Model Army revolver with its heavy octagon barrel.

"What the hell's going on?"

"Sheriff, I have two men to lodge in your jail. They're part of the Sam Bass gang of robbers who hit the Missouri & Texas Central express car three days ago down by Springfield."

"So?"

"So I want to leave them here for safekeeping while I chase the other four members of the gang."

"Don't think so."

"What was that?' Spur asked not believing his ears.

"Said, don't think so. No chance I'm gonna have them cluttering up my jail. Springfield, that's Greene county. Out of my jurisdiction. These boys do anything illegal in my county I'll be more than happy to arrest them. If they didn't, I can't help you."

"You're an elected peace officer, Sheriff. It's your responsibility to assist other law enforcement officers to catch and hold wanted felons regardless of the jurisdiction. Now open the door and get out your jail cell keys."

"Who the hell are you, mister?" Sheriff Parcheck asked.

"My name is Spur McCoy, and I have jurisdiction here. Let's put these men away and I'll show you my authorization."

"Nope. That's not what I got elected to do. Take them two back to Springfield yourself, if you got the grit. Me, I'm gonna get me about three more hours of sleep."

The door banged closed in Spur's face, the lock clicked in place and before Spur could pound on the wood, a bar slid into holders inside.

"Told you," one of the prisoners said. "Told you old Lund wouldn't hold no truck with you. Now what you gonna do, smartass lawman?"

"Shoot you I guess," Spur said thumbing back the hammer on his .45. "You two was shot and killed dead while trying to escape."

"Hold on now!" the drunk said, suddenly sober as a frosty mountain morning.

"He's joshing us," the wounded man said. "He ain't about to shoot us down in cold blood. His kind never do."

"You going to bet your life on that idea?" Spur asked softly. "I won't do it here. Wait until we get out of town a mile. Nobody will see, nobody will hear, nobody gonna know. Now move it, dogbreath! Let's walk out of town and north a ways. I want this wrapped up before the sun shows."

The former drunk stayed sober. He watched over his shoulder as Spur prodded him forward down the street and out of town.

"If I had my piece you wouldn't be doing this,"

the ex-drunk said.

"If I was you, robber man, I'd be worrying about the hereafter, whether there is one or not," Spur snorted. "You try to figure out just how your bullet riddled skull is going to fit into that after life picture."

"Man's got a soul," the wounded man said. "Everybody knows that. It ain't no part of the body, goes right on living."

"You don't say?" Spur said. "You be sure to come back from the dead and explain it all to me. Over there, down through that little swale and up into them shortleaf pine and that mess of white oak. Looks like a damn good place for an an attempted escape to me. A man would just naturally have to shoot to kill a prisoner trying to run for it."

Spur had made his camp in the thicket, and heard his horse whinny as they came up to it. The drunk was getting wild-eyed and Spur was worried he might try something stupid.

"Next to the tree," Spur told the shorter ex-drunk. "Sit down and put your hands behind you."

Spur cut his hand free where they were in front, and tied them in back of him, then tied him to the tree with two tight wraps on a shorter rope. Any more turns around the tree would give too much room to stretch the rope.

He tied the second man the same way to another tree ten feet away. "Stay comfortable, jail birds. I'll have you on your way to Springfield and a real sheriff just as soon as it gets dark. Want to be sure Sam and the rest of his boys didn't follow us."

As Spur turned toward town a piercing, agonizing inhuman scream slammed through the pine trees. It was a sound he had heard too often before, the cry of a horse in deadly peril. He dropped to the ground and rolled behind a tree just as half a dozen pistol shots thundered through the brush and trees from the direction where he had left his horse.

The two prisoners were laughing.

"Come on, Sam!" one of the tied men shouted.

"Sam, you got him belly-crawling to get away!" the wounded man yelled.

Well placed shots gave Spur no choice, he had to move backwark, away from the camp, away from his two captives. He only had his .45 with him. He fired and moved, fired and moved until he got to a big shortleaf pine that he could stand behind. He saw a man dart in toward the captives. By the time Spur shot at him it was too late.

Gunfire boomed beyond the bound men and slugs slammed into Spur's protective tree.

Spur moved again, to the left to another tree for a better field of fire, but when he looked back at his camp, both the men from the robber band had been cut free and were gone.

A closing flurry of shots came toward his position, and then only silence. Spur did a cautious circle route moving back to check on his horse. Far away on the downslope toward town he saw four horses galloping away. Two of them were double loaded. So that's how Sam Bass had trailed him and beat him to the camp.

Spur crashed through the brush to his horse. The animal lay on her side. The grass had been pawed bare where her feet had thrashed in a death agony. Bright red blood painted the whole brushy area around her where blood had sprayed out after her neck had been sliced open.

Spur walked to his camp, picked up everything he had come with including his saddle, and selected a new campsite where he could see the approaches to

Branson and still stay under cover.

Almost all of the Ozark Mountains here were forested with the pines or one of five or six varieties of oak trees. Small valleys and stream gullies were clear and showed some grass, but the man had been right, this was not prime cattle country.

He sat there watching the town. There was no sign that the men he had just seen would ride out of Branson, but Spur knew that a man like Sam Bass would not risk a second confrontation. He had a reputation for clearing out fast, laying low, hiding out and staying inconspicuous between his raids. Maybe that was why he was so successful.

He would be gone as soon as he could get his gang together, get provisions and move out. Which meant Spur had to follow them. He picked up his saddle, Henry repeating rifle, and threw his saddlebags over his shoulder. He'd come back here for the rest. First he needed another horse, one without a slit throat.

McCoy was a big man at six feet two. He usually weighed in at two hundred pounds in his best fighting trim. It was all muscle, kept lean and hard by long days in the saddle and nights sleeping in a blanket on the hard ground.

He was tanned to a turn, had reddish brown hair and always wore a medium-crowned Stetson, this time a dark brown one and always with a string of silver Mexican pesos strung around the headband. His blue shirt was open at the collar and a stained and well lived-in brown leather vest showed one bullet hole and two grazes.

His hair was longer than that of most men, fighting with his collar and deep on each side with modified mutton chop sideburns. He wore a neatly trimmed half inch wide moustache to keep his upper lip warm. Dark green eyes stared out at Branson with a critical eye.

What kind of a town would elect a sheriff who would not help out another lawman? Spur intended to find out, and to give the man a large piece of his thinking on the subject before he took off trailing Sam Bass. There had to be more to it than simply a lazy sheriff who didn't know the job he was supposed to be doing.

Seeing Sheriff Parcheck was the first item on Spur's list as he trudged into town and dropped his saddle at the livery stable.

"Be back in a few minutes to pick out a horse to buy," Spur told a middle aged wrangler. "You find two of your best for me to take a look at."

"Yes sir," the man said. "What happened to your other horse?"

"She had a bit of a circulation problem. All of her blood ran out a wide slice across her throat. Any more questions?"

The wrangler's eyes opened wide and he shook his head.

# 4

Spur McCoy marched out of the livery stable and straight to the county sheriff's small office where he banged through the door and stared at Sheriff Parcheck who worked on a plateful of fried eggs, hashbrowns, bacon and a big cup of coffee.

"Yeah?" the sheriff said looking up. "Oh, it's you again, the big federal lawman. You must be federal to claim you have jurisdiction in my county. So you catch the rest of them?"

"You know damn well I didn't. You probably also know I lost the first two, and I'm holding you responsible. I'll be sending a telegram to the Missouri State Attorney General as soon as I can. I'll have you removed from office."

"Don't say. Give my regards to Butch Dolan, he's the attorney general, good buddy of mine. Anything else on your mind? You're holding up my breakfast."

"Do the important things first, Sheriff. Right now you are violating your state oath of office, aiding and abetting a known felon and half a dozen more charges I'll have ready. The Sam Bass gang is probably out of town by now. They were staying in the old Parsons place and you knew it."

"Might have. Might not. Hard to prove what a man knows. You any real business with me? If not I see a young feller who has a real problem."

Spur turned and saw a tall, slender man in a black suit and string tie standing in the doorway.

"If I lose Sam Bass's trail, I'll be back, Sheriff. And you aren't going to be pleased with what happens when I get here." Spur pointed his finger at the sheriff, stabbed it twice at him in emphasis, then spun and walked toward the door.

As he came to the young man he saw a determined, angry look, and knew it must be a mirror of his own. The man walked past and stood in front of the sheriff's desk, his fists balled and placed angrily on hips.

"I see you've managed to kill Frank Davis and not make a ripple in the whole town. Well, I for one, won't stand for it."

"Russell," the Sheriff said in a growning, pained voice. "We've been over this a dozen times. I've told you, bring me some real evidence of foul play and we'll have a look see at the whole situation. It was a house fire, for Christ's sakes. People die all the time when their stoves overheat."

"True, but this one got some help. I found two five gallon coal oil cans just outside the burned out frame of Frank's place. That was before some of your men took them away and destroyed them."

"Those are real bad charges you're making, son. Don't care if you are a damn lawyer. Hell, I could sue you for slander or something. Now you get your ass out of here, and I don't want to hear another word about Frank Davis. You do, and I won't be able to protect you."

"Same way you couldn't protect Frank, right, Sheriff? I don't see how you people keep on doing it, year after year."

"Just upholding the law., Maybe you didn't read for the law long enough, boy. You got a damn lot to learn about practical application of the law. Now get, before I jail you right now!"

Spur had stood at the door in plain sight of both men as the argument went on, now he stepped outside and waited for the young lawyer.

When the man came out, Spur held out his hand.

"I'm Spur McCoy, new to town. Heard your session with the sheriff in there."

"Phillip Russell, attorney-at-law, for all the good it does in this town. My suggestion, sir, is don't stay, ride straight through and then shake any dust off your boots from this county so it doesn't contaminate anyone else."

"Sheriff is a bit high handed?"

"No, inactive. He doesn't do a thing except draw his pay and eat three meals a day. He has no deputies. He never arrests anyone, he looks the other way when a man is gunned down in the streets, hanged outside his house or burned up in his bed. I think he's in with them somehow, but I can't figure how."

"In with them? What do you mean?"

The young man shook his head. "You don't want to get mixed up in this. Here in Branson we have the craziest law set-up I've ever seen. There's no district attorney for the county. They had one but he was run out of town about five years ago, the way I hear. They simply haven't got around to electing a new one.

"There is no kind of local judge. Old Judge Filmore died two years ago, and nobody wanted to run for office. Once in a while a circuit judge comes through, but he usually goes hunting with some of the boys, or catches up on his fishing down at the lake.

"The sheriff is an absolute loon. He knows nothing about law or law enforcement and is proud of the fact. He simply does nothing. But he is good friends with the people at the state capitol up at Jefferson City. Goes up there two or three times a year and comes back sassy as the dickens.

"I've only been here about three months, and everything here is strange. I shouldn't be bothering you about it."

"No, I'm interested. Maybe we should talk some more."

"I have some people to talk to this morning," Russell said. "A will to set up actually. I'll be free right after noon. Come to my office, that's at my small house just two doors down from the little church. I've got a shingle out."

Spur rubbed his chin. "Tell you what. I have to make a run at finding Sam Bass. If I lose him, I'll be back this way."

The two men shook hands and Spur watched him for a moment, then hurried over to the general store and began stocking up on some provisions for a long ride. He had no idea what direction Sam Bass would take. If he headed on South into Arkansas it would be a rough, lonesome ride.

Sam might point for Fayetteville or Little Rock. He would steer around Fort Smith and Judge Parker, the hanging judge.

"Let's see," the store man said. "We got coffee, salt, dry beans, six cans of peaches, slab of bacon, cornmeal, dried apples and apricots and five pounds of raisins. You must be planning on doing a mite of hunting along the way."

"Peers as how," Spur said. He paid the bill of four dollars and thirty-seven cents, and carried it all out of the store in an empty five pound floor sack the man sold for a nickel.

At the livery he checked over two horses. He liked a bay mare the best. She was broad across the chest and like a typical quarter horse, higher in the rear quarters than the front. She looked like she could hit a stride and hold it all day. He saddled her and took her around the block. When he came back he was satisfied. She was smooth, responsive and as calm as a small frog floating on a large lily pad.

"Thirty dollars," the stable owner said. He was a big man, with a fat belly and wore bib overalls so he didn't have to use a belt. He waddled rather than walked and had a birthmark on his right cheek of bright purple.

"Give you twenty, which is five more than she's worth," Spur said. They dickered a dollar at a time and settled on twenty-five, what she was worth and what both were thinking about as the right price all the time. But both were now happy and had the fun of horse trading a little.

Spur tied on his sack of provisions, pushed the Henry into the cross boot and tied it in place with a quick pull loop that made the weapon available to one hand in about three seconds.

He rode to the Parsons place and checked inside. The house was a mess, broken bottles, leftovers of food, and the look of a quick exit by all concerned. The fancy women were gone. He found a hat and a shirt, some female undergarments and one half empty bottle of whiskey.

In the back yard he located dozens of hoof prints. Two of the horses were shod, the others weren't.

Unusual. He moved out to the street and checked and found the same shod/unshod group of prints leading to the south and out of town.

The tracks were easy to follow the first quarter mile on the dirt street, then a country road. There the last signs of civilization ended and the open country took over. Spur rode ahead fifty yards and made a sweeping arc around the end of the trail. He picked up the hoof prints at the far side of the ride. The trail led southwest and Spur followed.

He used the quick trail method he used for long range tracking. Spur figured they were heading out for a far run, so he rode a hundred yards ahead on the general pointing of the trail, then crisscrossed the area until he found the trail again. If the direction left only one good route, he could ride a half mile ahead before he made his arc to find the prints again.

Spur worked for two hours this way, moving up slopes on the Ozark mountains, through sparse growths of oak, and then heavier stands of shortleaf pine. Here the tracking was easier because of the leaf mulch on the ground that left good hoof tracks.

He came over a brow of a ridge and angled down only to find himself on a rocky reverse slope of shale. There was no chance to find tracks here. He rode down the shale to the small stream below, then turned southwest on the far side of the six inch deep water and searched for tracks.

After a half mile of moving downstream he found nothing. He turned and rode upstream, retracing his tracks, then working a mile up the small creek. Nowhere did he find tracks showing that the six men had crossed the stream.

He went back up the shale to the top and found where the riders had hit the rocky area. Now he searched laterally. The shale slope ran for two miles one direction. There were small rock slides and fresh marks on some of the rocky formations, but he had no way of knowing if they were made by Sam Bass's gang.

Spur checked back the other way. The shale slope vanished into vegetation after half a mile ahead but there were no signs that any horsemen had come off the shale onto the oak tree spotted landscape.

The Secret Agent sat on his bay with a feeling of frustration. In the years of working the West he had developed into an excellent tracker. It infuriated him that Sam Bass and his men had outsmarted him. Now he rode back the opposite way to the end of the slate, and now found another rocky formation extending all the way into the water. They could have moved down the stream.

Again Spur followed the brook downstream. He worked one side for a mile, then cut back and worked the other side. At no place was the water too deep for the horses to wade through.

Twice he worked additional mile stretches, and on the third he found a spot the horses had left the water. They had moved at a gallop then, he could tell by the marks in the soft under footing.

Spur followed them to a rise and looked down. There was a wagon road leading from a small sawmill that was turning the larger white oak into saw lumber. Most of it would probably end as flooring.

The problem was the road headed south, out of the mill and he was sure into Arkansas toward the nearest large town. As he watched he saw two wagons each pulled by a team of six move along the road.

The hoof prints and the wagon wheels of just one

such rig would wipe out any chance Spur might have had of following the Sam Bass gang. He had lost them this time for sure.

It was nearly four in the afternoon when Spur turned back north. He still wanted to talk to the young lawyer. There had to be more than met the eye in this small Ozark mountain town. The coal oil fire where a man was burned to death? That type of murder seemed remarkably similar to one other Spur could recall.

It would take him two hours to ride back to town. Spur turned the bay's head to the north and began to ride.

Back in Branson Phillip Russell stood in his small "office" which was in reality his living room converted with a desk and some files and a table. Three men stood across the room from him. All three wore white hoods with small slits for eyes and mouth. His wife huddled beside him. Right then Phillip was glad they had no children.

"I don't understand this at all," Phillip said. "I am a lawyer and representing the dead man's family. We are going to sue the county for a hundred thousand dollars for allowing law and order to become so lax that a band of vigilantes killed this man and set his house on fire to cover up the crime."

"Not a chance!" the middle sized man thundered. "Shoulda stayed where you was 'fore you come here."

"Shut up," a shorter man growled. He had a big belly and a silver buckle in the shape of a big "C." "Too damn much talk. Russell, you been found guilty by the Branson People's Justice Committee and been sentenced to hang."

"No, no, no!" Priscilla screamed from behind Russell. She was a slender woman with soft reddish hair, light skin and dimples in her cheeks. Now her eyes blazed. "You are killers, murderers! You can't walk in here and drag my husband off. There are laws!"

The third man jumped beside Priscilla Russell, grabbed her by the shoulders and pushed her across the room. Phillip started to protest, but the short, heavy set man pushed a six-gun muzzle under his chin and shoved it upward.

The soft tissue drove higher and Phillip lifted his head to lessen the intense pain.

"Leave her alone!" Phillip shouted. "Let her be! This is my doing, not hers!"

The chubby man nodded his hood and the third man with a sawed off shutgun, pushed the woman into a chair and held out his hand to warn her to stay there.

The fat man chuckled. "Yes, now I'd say we have better order in the court here. The lawyer has appealed his sentence. Appeals judge, do you have your ruling on his case yet?"

The third man laughed and Priscilla noticed that when he turned one of his legs was weak and he limped. She knew who did that in town if only she could remember, a limp. Who limped?

"Fact is, Mr. Executioner, this court has come to a decision. The appeal is denied, and the original sentence for Mr. Russell is hereby reinstated, and be carried out immediately."

"Well now, peers we done all we could for the condemned man. Gone through the legalities, and all." The fat man eased the six-gun away from Phillip's chin and pressed the muzzle against the lawyer's heart.

"Inside or outside?" the shorter, rotund man asked.

Priscilla knew she had to keep her wits. They were going to kill Phillip. There wasn't anything she could do about it. She hated them! But she would get even. The man with the limp, she could find him. The short, fat one, his belt buckle said "C." Where had she seen it? Then she remembered, outside the saloon. The man owned one of the saloons, the Cat's Claw, she thought they called it. But the other one, the tall, thin man. She had no idea about him. He hadn't said a word.

Priscille began unbuttoning the flowered print blouse she wore over the long skirt.

"I have another appeal," she said loudly. By the time the three men looked at her the blouse was hanging loose in front of her open to the bottom. "I have an offer," she went on. Calmly she shrugged out of the blouse. The white cotton chemise hung over her shoulders by thin straps and covered her breasts.

"No!" Phillip thundered. "Damnit, Priscilla, no!"

The shorter man slashed his .44 six-gun across Phillip's head, slamming him back a step, leaving a trail of blood across his forehead.

"Shut up, you! I want to see what the little lady is offering," the short vigilante said.

"I offer myself, for the life of my husband. Now, and anytime in the future." She lifted the chemise with both hands and pulled it off over her head. Her full breasts rolled and bounced for a moment from the motion. They were large, with heavy pink nipples and darker shade pink areolas four inches across.

"Damn, look at them tits!" the tall man who hadn't spoken, said. He had a slight lisp and

Priscilla knew at once who he was, Barney Figuroa, a clerk in one of the stores in town. She had bought groceries from him often.

"Beautiful," the short man said. He moved to her and cupped one breast with his hand.

"All three of you, twice each, right now in the bedroom. Tie up Phillip. When you're all through, you leave, and Phillip and I ride out of town within an hour. Agreed?"

Priscilla could hear the short man's breath come in quick gasps. He rubbed her breast and she hated it, but she would gladly bed them to save her husband's life. The short man reached for his crotch and unbuttoned the fasteners.

"Right here, right now!" he said.

"Shit no!" the man with the limp bellowed. "Damnit, we can get all the pussy we want, anytime. Stop it! We got a job to do here, not worry about our puds!"

The short man jumped back as if he had been slapped. He shook his head inside the hood, and then let out a long sigh.

"Yeah, damnit, you're right. But look at them beauties! I always did go for real redheads. Bet she's got red pussy hair, too!'"

"Let's do it," the man with the slight lisp said. He pulled cord from his pocket and started to tie Phillip's hands. Phillip kicked out trying for his crotch, but missed and the man knocked down Phillip with one punch. Two of them tied Phillip's hands and lifted him to his feet.

The short man fondled Priscilla's breasts again, then sighed. "Mrs. Russell, you put your clothes back on. I got to tie you up for a bit here."

Two minutes later she was tied to the chair and they had a hangman's knot noose tightened around

Phillip's neck. They led him out the back door.

Two of them boosted Phillip into a bareback horse, then they all mounted horses they had left and rode to the front of the house where a big black oak forty foot high grew. Now they worked quickly, efficiently.

One man threw the half inch hemp rope over a slanting limb, caught the end and tied it around the trunk. The second man had walked Phillip's horse so he was directly under where the rope went over the limb.

The rope was pulled tight around the trunk and all slack taken up.

As this took place, the short fat man rode a block up the street and walked his mount back, firing his six-gun and shot at a time until it was empty. Then he shouted.

"Execution! Execution! Execution! Everyone come and see the execution of a law breaker and a man who is a threat to this stable and prosperous community!"

By the time he walked his horse back to the Russell house, forty people had left stores and saloons and followed him. A dozen children raced around pointing to the man on the horse with the noose around his neck.

"Bad man! Bad man! Bad man!" they chanted in unison.

When the people were gathered around, the leader nodded and the tall man with the lisp pushed the point of his knife a half inch into the horse's rump. The animal cried out in pain, dug in her back haunches and shot forward in a mighty stride to get away from the pain.

Phillip Russell jolted off the bare back of the horse. He dropped to the end of the slack in the rope and witnesses heard a crack as his neck broke. The horse rushed down the street heading out of town.

Phillip Russell hung by his neck and a hush came over the crowd. His feet twitched with muscle spasms. His eyes came open and his vacant, dead stare seemed to fasten on each witness. His hands twitched and then the three hooded figures looked at one another.

They all fired rounds into the air, then raced their horses down the street and around to the other side of town.

Priscilla Russell heard the first shots, the harangue. She tore at the rope trying to get untied. She could hear the rustle of skirts and the chatter of the people. Then she had the ropes undone and rushed to the window.

"Noooooooooo!" she screamed. She saw Phillip sitting on the horse. Priscilla rushed to the front door and down the steps, not remembering that she had not buttoned her blouse. She saw the horse surge away from Phillip and saw him slide off the rump of the animal and then fall.

Priscilla screamed and a woman looked at her and rushed up just as she fell. Priscilla was unconscious when her husband's neck broke and he died. The woman lowered Priscilla to the spring grass and fanned her.

Down the street, Spur McCoy rode into town after his futile search for Sam Bass. He saw the man hanging by his neck and pulled his pistol and charged down the two blocks to where a dozen people still stood looking up at the gently swaying corpse.

Spur saw no men left around the hanging. Only a few children and three women who were sitting on the grass with what seemed to be an unconscious woman. He saw that the house stood two down from the church and scowled as he waited for the body to turn around on the rope.

Then he saw what he had feared. The dead man was Phillip Russell, the young lawyer who had argued with the sheriff, the man Spur wanted to talk to. Spur swung down from the horse. From up the street he saw the sheriff approaching on foot.

# 5

Spur went to the women sitting on the ground and looked at the grandmother who held the unconscious lady.

"Is this Mrs. Russell?" Spur asked.

"Yes, and my friend, and I don't want you to hurt her no more!" The older lady pushed out her chin in defiance.

The sheriff walked past them without a glance in their direction and looked at the body turning slowly on the half inch hemp rope.

Spur stood and walked over where he could face the lawman by looking past the body.

"Nice work, Sheriff. You certainly prevented this vigilante murder, didn't you? Your really have a talent for law enforcement. I'm back, told you I might come back. Just what in hell is going on in your county?"

"Fact is, you're right. This is my county. You hit the nail right on the head with the old hammer. Now, you want to help me cut down this poor soul, or you want to stand there yammering while the widow is over there crying her eyes out?"

Spur flipped out a knife, reached over the dead man's head, sliced the half inch hemp in two, then caught Phillip Russell's body and lowered it to the ground. He put the knife away and kept staring at the sheriff.

"Can't say as if you've heard the last of this, Sheriff. Can't say that at all." Spur turned and walked away down the street and around the corner. He watched the death scene through a bush near the house. The sheriff called to two men passing by and had them carry the body to a wagon which hauled it away. Mrs. Russell revived and went into her house with one of the women.

Spur went down the block, around it and up the alley in back of the Russell house. He needed to talk to the widow, findout what she knew about this place.

He needed some answers from Mrs. Russell about her husband. Spur knocked on the back door, and one of the women he had seen comforting Mrs. Russell opened the screen.

"Yes?"

"I wondered if I could speak with Mrs. Russell? I was a friend of her husband."

"Not now. Land sakes," the older woman said, anger in her voice. "Priscilla just became a widow! You should have a little respect."

"Are you her friend?"

"Why, yes, I guess I am."

"I want to find out who killed her husband and why. I want to know more about this town, this county, and especially about the sheriff. I figure she can tell me."

"Jesus, Joseph and Mary, I hope so!" The gray haired woman pushed open the screen and motioned. "Come in, come in. I ain't seen a man in this town with that glint in his eye and that set to his jaw for a year. My own husband was killed about a year ago. Same bunch. They've taken over the whole county. Won't put up with no outsiders. Phillip and Priscilla are outsiders and they didn't like it one bit."

"Somebody is holding everyone in this whole county as prisoners?"

"More or less, you might say. I'm Wilma. I put Priscilla down in her bed for a minute, but I'm sure she'll want to talk with you. Let me go see her. First off I thought you was from the funeral parlor. You just wait."

Spur sat on the small couch in the living room. It was a spartan house with little furniture, but with family pictures on the wall and a "God Bless This House" needlepoint framed near the front door. It was a poor house, but with warmth and honesty about it.

A few minutes later, Wilma came out of the far door, and a young, red haired woman followed her. Her eyes were red and her cheeks flushed. One hand went to her hair selfconsciously. She was slight, not more than five feet three inches tall and wouldn't weigh as much as a sack of potatoes.

Wilma motioned at Spur. "This is the gentleman, Priscilla. I think he wants to help. Nobody else in town is going to lift a finger, you know that. You've seen it happen before. Now I got to get on over to the hotel and get the food started for the evening meal. I'd say you can trust this young man."

She smiled at them, then hurried out the front door and down the two steps to the sidewalk.

Spur stood with his mid-crowned hat in his hands. Priscilla was a pretty girl, maybe twenty-five, and the soft red hair he noticed before had been combed carefully. Now her fingers were tightened into fists hanging at her sides. She looked angry and scared and furious all at once.

"Wilma didn't know your name," Priscilla said, her voice soft, lower than he would have guessed. "I'm Priscilla Russell. The Widow Russell, now I reckon."

"Ma'am. My name is Spur McCoy."

"Mr. McCoy, please sit down. Wilma said you had talked with Phillip?"

"This morning. I was supposed to come back and see him just after lunch. I was interested in the sheriff. Now I'm even more interested and worried. Couldn't the sheriff have stopped the lynching?"

"Of course, but he knows his place. The people who run the county tell him what to do."

"Even to stand by during a lynching?"

"Yes, and worse. But you have one thing wrong, Mr. McCoy. My huband was not lynched, he was murdered. Those three men came in here with guns and tied me to a chair and bound Phillip's hands behind his back, then pushed him out the back door. They murdered him."

"Mrs. Russell, that sounds almost impossible here in this day and age. It's the late eighteen seventies. This isn't eighteen fifty anymore. Still I got here just after it happened. This morning, early, I tried to get the sheriff to hold two train robbers for me and he wouldn't do it. I think you better tell me exactly what is going on in this county, and who is behind it. Can you do that?"

Priscilla Russell nodded. "First, let me make you some coffee, we're both going to need some. This story is going to take some time."

They sat across a tiny kitchen table and held steaming mugs of coffee. Spur worked on a fresh baked cinnamon roll. Priscilla took a deep breath.

"I want you to know that life is cheap in this county. I'm probably signing my own death warrant by telling you this, but somebody has to. Since Phillip is . . . gone . . . there isn't a lot left I want to live for anyway.

"We came up here from Springfield about four months ago. Phil knew there wasn't a lawyer here, and he figured there would be plenty of civil law for him to keep busy. He didn't figure on the Bald Knobbers."

Spur frowned. "I'm sorry, Mrs. Russell. I don't understand. You said the Bald Knobbers?"

"Yes. A group not well known except in Tane county here and the next county to the west, Stone. We learned about them in a rush the first couple of weeks we were here. A man was dragged out of a saloon downtown and shot dead by four hooded men. They chased the poor soul, used him as target practice.

"Phillip never carried a gun. He ran out and yelled at the men, but they only laughed and shot into the dirt at Phil's feet so he had to dance. One of the bullets took the heel off his boot. Phil began asking around and learned about the Bald Knobbers that same day. He told me. I figured that Phillip could live with it. Turned out he couldn't.

"The whole thing began during the Civil War when the border raiders from both the North and the South swept through this state and up into Kansas. They called themselves patriots, stealing and looting and gathering gold and supplies for one army or the other.

"But most of the men in both those groups were simply outlaws, criminals, misfits who couldn't stand it to be in the regular army. The Border

Raiders like Quantrel and his men made life unbearable in two or three states for two or three years.

"When the war ended the raiders disbanded, most of them. Some of them became outlaws and went right on doing what they had been doing. Others settled down. A lot of them came to roost here in Taney county.

"There wasn't a lot of law here in the best of times. We're cut off way down here. The state government kind of forgot us. The locals run things to suit themselves.

"It began as a fine, upstanding form of self rule. If the judge didn't come through, some of the townsfolk would elect a judge, and the best men in the community would sit on the jury and they would take care of the disputes and what few criminals who blundered in here. Seemed to work.

"Gradually the self governing became the only kind of law we had around here, and it became ingrown but just and a fine practical system. Then over the years the high principled men who began the whole thing died off or faded from the scene.

"Finally the men who ran things did away with the trials. The men gathered and decided who was good for the community and who wasn't, and the bad ones were run out of the county.

"If the people involved didn't want to go, they were encouraged. The men in power began wearing hoods to keep their identity secret and make it a pure vigilante function so no one could be blamed."

Priscilla sipped at her hot coffee.

"Power corrupts. Absolute power corrupts absolutely."

She looked up at Spur. "You've done some reading. I've heard that. It certainly was true here. Ten years after the war was over the power in these two counties was firmly in the hands of the hooded men who enforced it.

"They became known as the Bald Knobbers. I don't know where the name came from or what it means. But all too soon the men in the hoods were hanging and burning, and running people out of the county who they didn't like. Many times this was on a whim or a personal opinion of one man. It was often done to help one of the Knobbers financially.

"The merchants and property owners all joined the Bald Knobbers so they could protect themselves and their property. Now, thirteen years after the war is over, the Knobbers are riding as strong as ever.

"I know that Phillip thought he could do something to slow them down here. That was all he talked about. He knew the Knobbers were close friends with the state officials. He thought the Knobbers were making payoffs to the state people so they would not investigate the stories they got once in a while from down here.

"That's about it, Mr. McCoy. The Knobbers do whatever they want to. Kill . . . whoever gets in their way. Burn out the businessman who won't pay the 'dues' they insist on. I don't know what can stop them now. Phillip surely couldn't."

"And Sheriff Parcheck?" Spur asked. "How does he fit in?"

"However the Knobbers want him to. He has his orders. He is a figurehead. Goes to the state capitol at Jefferson City twice a year I'm told with a satchel filled with money. He's spineless, that's why the Knobbers ran him for sheriff. There was no one running against him."

"Both counties are in their grasp," Spur said. "So Springfield is the closest real law."

"Yes, but don't count on Sheriff Lacy there to help any. He's almost as afraid of the Knobbers as the folks around here are. He'd just say it's out of his jurisdiction and aim you at Jefferson City and the State Militia."

Priscilla stood. "I better get some supper. I always do. Would you stay and have supper with me? I'd appreciate it. I don't know if those men will come back or not."

"Mrs. Russell, I think I can be here for a while. Is there someone you could stay with for a few days, especially over tonight?"

"No. Just Wilma, the woman who was here when you came. She works till late, then usually takes a room at the hotel. Don't worry about it, Mr. McCoy. I'll get by."

She went to the counter and began peeling potatoes. "I was planning on steaks for supper. Put them in the ice box last night and they're still good. Would that be all right?"

"Yes, of course. I'll be getting a room at the hotel. I'm going to be staying a few days."

She looked up quickly. "Hotel might not be the best idea."

"Why's that?"

"Your argument with the sheriff. Man who owns the hotel is a Knobber. The sheriff probably has told everyone how you stood up to him and that you're an outsider and causing trouble." She blinked back tears.

"Lordy, I don't want you getting hurt because you helped me."

"Don't plan on getting hurt, Mrs. Russell."

She turned, tears streaming down her face. "I almost saved Phillip, did I tell you that? I knew they were going to kill him. I offered myself to them. I took off my blouse and my . . . my chemise so I was bare on top and told them I'd make love to them if right afterwards Phillip and I could leave."

"That was brave."

"No, desperate! I wanted to save my husband. One of them would have but then the other two shamed him out of it. It was so close! I knew the three men. I'm going to get even with them, even if it kills me. I'm going to shoot them down, Mr. McCoy. Does that surprise you?"

"No. Grief has a way of changing people. But let me handle this. I have some law enforcement connections. I should be able to take care of the whole thing and not endanger you."

She worked over the wooden cook stove for a few more minutes and Spur smelled the delicious aroma of cooking steak. Soon she had the meal on the table, with warmed up cinnamon rolls, steak, potatoes, fresh peas, applesauce, and lots of hot coffee.

Twenty minutes later, Spur pushed back from the table and grinned.

"Best home cooked meal I've had in months, Mrs. Russell. Now I really do have to go look for a hotel room. If I don't I'll be sleeping on the hard ground for another night."

She touched his shoulder. "Mr. McCoy. I want to tell you who the three men are who murdered my husband. One of them is Abe Conners, he's a short little man about forty, who is chunky fat and owns a saloon called the Cat's Claw. I think he's also the head man in the Knobbers, but I'm not sure.

"The tall man was Barney Figuroa. He has a slight lisp and works as a clerk at the Branson General Store. The third one was Vern Smith, our friendly town banker. Only one here. Two other bankers had 'accidents' caused by the Knobbers.

Vern Smith also has a slight limp."

Spur listened, his concern for the woman growing. "Mrs. Russell, I hope that you won't do anything for a few days. Let me see what I can find out, what I can do. Will you promise me that?"

"I just want them to pay!"

"They'll pay for their crimes. I'm the one to see to that. Oh, do you have a gun in the house? You might need it for protection."

She went to a drawer in the writing desk in the living room and brought out an old .44. Spur checked it and saw that it had five rounds in it. He took them out and examined them. They were new and the weapon worked.

"Can you shoot a gun?"

"No, show me how."

"All you have to do is hold it with both hands, aim down the barrel and pull the trigger. Never point it at anyone unless you are ready to kill them. Maybe sometime later we can practice shooting it."

"Yes, I want to practice. I have a reason now."

Spur watched her, decided the reason was for her own protection, and let it pass. "Tell me about your husband. Did he think he might be in danger?"

"Yes, from the first time he raised his voice against the unlawfulness. We talked about leaving and moving back to Springfield. I just wish to god that we had done it!"

Tears brimmed her eyes.

"They are going to pay for killing Phillip, Mr. McCoy, I promise you that."

"The law will handle it, Mrs. Russell. If we try to take the law into our own hands, how are we any better than they are?"

She wiped the tears away. Her soft cheeks pale, strands of the red hair hanging limply over one eye.

She pushed the hair back and her face took on a harder, stronger look.

"Mr. McCoy, I might not look it, but I can be as tough as I need to be. The people in this town don't know the real me, but they will before they hear the last of me. I promise them that!"

Spur frowned. "About tonight. You want me to come up the alley and slip in the back door? Nobody else would know I was here. I'll sleep on the couch and you can lock your bedroom door. I owe you for the good dinner."

She shook her head. "No, Spur McCoy, you take care of your hide tonight. That sheriff is going to be telling the Knobbers stories about you."

The big Secret Agent watched the pretty woman a moment, then agreed with her. "They can tell stories, but I can do the same thing. Now, I better get down the street and find a hotel room for the night. I can help you pack if you want to get ready to move back to Springfield. Better you get out of town as soon as you can."

"Not me, McCoy. I have some special business to attend to first."

Spur watched her for a minute, the glint in her eyes was plain to see, and Spur knew she was going to cause trouble in Branson.

# 6

Spur walked the two blocks from the Russell house to the middle of the row of stores on his way to the small hotel. Spur had not thought much about it until he saw a black family coming down the street. Now he realized the little town was about one third black.

He was in the south, a south still smarting over the Civil War and the freedom of the Negroes. He watched as the five in the black family stepped off the boardwalk and let an older white man and woman walk past. Spur was simply not used to this kind of action. No one told the Negroes to get off the sidewalk, they just did it from long practice, and perhaps local custom.

He continued up the street and saw a black woman ahead of him. She was standing on the boardwalk staring at a white woman who held a parasol and a sneer on her face.

As Spur walked up he could hear catcalls coming and various voices raised in jeers. The black woman was in her mid twenties, the white woman in her forties. They stood and stared at each other.

At last the white woman sniffed. "I am certainly not going to move to let some black no account like you walk past," she said.

The black woman snorted. "Well I sure ain't gonna get my bones off the boards just so some white no account old battle axe like you can step all over my pride."

"Girl, you should be horsewhipped!" the woman snapped. She motioned at the storefront nearby. "Will, you get out here and teach this chippy a leason or two? Just too uppity, she is for her own good."

Two white men came from the store, one had an apron around his waist, the other one carried a short whip that had leather thongs knotted on the ends and a two foot handle.

"Some trouble here?" the apron man asked.

"This . . . this . . . creature refused to let me walk along the sidewalk," the white woman spat.

The black woman looked at the white man. "This is none of your business, mister."

"Making it my business," he said and stepped forward. With his crossed arms, he pushed the black woman off the boardwalk into the dusty street. He waved the white woman past and then stared down at the black.

"Black whore, you got a problem."

"I am not a whore," she snapped back. "But you look like a pimp!"

The man's face flushed. He turned and saw half a dozen other white man and a few blacks watching him. Somebody snickered. A woman giggled behind them.

"Hold on, black trash! You don't talk to Hirum Streib that way. You from the north?"

The black woman looked at Streib, then at the

others watching and began to back up slowly. She turned at last and ran for the other side of the street —and blundered directly into the waiting arms of two white men who had been watching. One man's hand caught her breast and he left his hand there.

"Lookie here what I got!" he shouted. A dozen men roared with laughter as they moved in behind Streib. The men across the street pushed the black girl ahead of them as they ushered her back to Hirum Streib.

When she came near the boardwalk a foot below Streib, the men stopped her, and Streib laughed.

"Black whore, you have a name?"

She ignored him.

"I said, black whore, you got a name?"

She spit in his face and Streib slapped her with his open palm. She would have fallen if one of the men behind her had not caught her.

"Too drunk to stand up!" somebody shouted.

"Little gal is top heavy. Look at them big tits!" one of the men catchers yelled. Everyone roared again. The black woman began to edge away, but Streib dropped off the foot-high boardwalk into the street beside her. His hand caught her blouse front and he jerked down suddenly.

The force of the motion pulled her shoulders down, but as she resisted, the seams of the material broke and the blouse ripped free at both shoulders and the whole front tore down below each arm. She had been wearing nothing under the blouse and was now bare to the waist. Her breasts showed large and uptilted nipples.

"Now, we got ourselves a real black whore!" Streib yelled. "How much am I offered for a quick roll in the hay with this black bitch?"

The woman did not try to hide her breasts. She

swung her hands instead, her fingernails raking down across Streib's cheek, digging four grooves which quickly filled with blood.

Streib roared in fury and swing his right fist at her jaw. She ducked under it and darted away. The two catchers grabbed her again, and Streib ran up to her in screaming fury.

A gunshot stopped the whole affair. Everyone turned and looked for the source and found Spur McCoy standing in the middle of the street.

"Let the lady alone and move back, or eat lead for supper!" Spur bellowed in his best army field command voice.

The catchers let go of the black woman.

Streib stared in amazement.

A dozen men on the boardwalk snorted in surprise.

"Move back!" Spur roared again, firing a round under the boardwalk. Whites and blacks scattered on both sides. Spur motioned to the woman with his left hand and she ran toward him. He and the woman edged back to the boardwalk on the far side of the street. Out of the corner of his eye Spur saw a man draw a weapon on his left.

Spur spun and fired, the round taking the gunman in the thigh and slamming him against the chairs in front of the General Store.

"Anyone else want a lead sandwich?" Spur shouted.

Nobody moved.

Spur backed toward the alley, then into the shadows there and caught the woman's hand and they ran hard down the alley and across the street and behind a row of houses.

Only then did the woman stop shaking.

Spur turned and looked at her. She still did not try

to hide her breasts. Spur slid out of a light jacket he had worn that morning and she put it on. Dusk was fast approaching.

"My name is Spur McCoy, and I have a feeling that you really are from the north. Right?"

The woman buttoned the jacket and looked up at Spur. "My name is Edith Washington. Yes, I'm from the north. I'm in town to try to find my brother. We last heard from him about six months ago when he stopped here."

"Edith, you are now in the south, where the people wish slavery was still legal. Did you get that feeling just now back there?"

"Yes." Tears began to seep from her eyes, then she was sobbing and Spur put his arms around her and held her a minute. She stopped a moment later and wiped her eyes.

'Sorry. I'm usually stronger than that. I seldom break up and cry. My mother was an extremely strong person. I have never been treated like that before. I'm from Philadelphia. My people have not been slaves for over a hundred years."

She moved away from him.

"Mr. McCoy, you must be a northerner, too. I know they'll try to run you out of town, or hire somebody to kill you. I'm almost certain that my brother, John, is dead. Somebody probably pushed him off the sidewalk, too, and he pushed back. John would do that."

She sighed. "Now I guess I'll have to go back home. They won't let me alone here now." She frowned and watched him. "That means we'll never know about John."

"I'll try to find out. Somebody must know. What about the black leaders in the town?"

"There aren't any. The few men here still act like they are slaves."

Edith shivered under his jacket. "What are you going to do now?"

"I was heading for the hotel to get a room for the night."

Edith laughed. "That room would become your grave. The man who runs the hotel is one of the Bald Knobbers."

"That's two people who have told me that, so it must be true. I guess I can camp out another night."

"Then you head back north. No sense dying down here."

"Might. But I'm also interested in who killed that young lawyer today."

"Mr. Russell. I talked with him about finding John. He was asking some questions for me."

"Edith, I can't go back and leave things this way. I'm going to do something about it. I'm not sure what."

"Then you'll need some help and a place to stay. I know a place out of town a ways, you'll be safe there. Get your horse and meet me behind the church in about half an hour."

"Why are you doing this, Edith?"

"Mr. McCoy, it . . ."

He held up his hands. "Hey, call me Spur. Enough of that mister stuff."

She smiled in the fading light. It would be full dark now in another ten minutes.

"Yes, all right. Spur, you probably saved my life back there. They start like that, the fights, the disturbances, then they get meaner and meaner and somebody suggests target practice . . . I saw it happen once about a month ago. They teased this cowboy who was just riding through. Teased him and made him mad, then they took his gun away . . . and killed him."

She shook her head as if to clear it. "Now, enough of this. You go get your gear, and your horse, and I'll meet you in half an hour. I'll be careful. I'll be safe enough on the black side of town."

She turned and walked into the darkness.

Spur lifted his brows. It might be good to have a local guide. At least he knew he could trust her. Spur moved down the street and went over a block to where he had left his horse near the Russell house.

He watched for ten minutes before he walked out to claim his mount, rifle and provisions. He could spot no one watching the horse, no one lurking in doorways. Spur mounted quickly and rode into the darkness, glad now for the protection. He wondered if Edith would come. There was nothing he could do now for the widow Russell. He'd check on her tomorrow.

Spur sat on his bay in the shadows behind the church, avoiding the moonlight. The only person he saw moving was a small boy running to the outhouse behind his home, banging the door, then a moment later racing through the dreaded darkness back to the safety of the shaft of yellow light from the back door.

Five minutes later Edith rode up beside him. She was dressed in men's pants, a blouse, a heavy jacket and a hat that hid her shoulder length black hair.

"Ready, Spur?"

"Am now."

Without another word, she turned her horse and rode. They moved north of town, higher on the slopes, out of the heavy oak timber into taller shortleaf pines.

They rode for half an hour. Spur guessed they were about two miles from the small town. They went into a valley no more than fifty yards wide. A hundred yards upstream on a tiny trickle of water they came to a log cabin.

The place was old, abandoned. The structure was twenty feet square, and the sturdy pine logs were notched carefully and fitted. They even had been well plastered where they met.

"Home sweet home," she said. "It isn't used much. Most folks don't know it's here. Some of us Negroes come up here to hide from the whites when they go on a rampage."

Inside, Spur found that the place had no windows. He snapped a match and was surprised to find a lamp full of kerosene and with a trimmed wick. He lit it.

The place had been cleaned recently. It had two bunks built against the wall with wire strung across them to serve as springs, the blue ticking mattress he guessed were filled with leaves or straw.

A table and a small fireplace stood at the far side.

Edith vanished outside, and Spur followed. He brought in his sack of provisions and she carried a sack from the back of her horse. In it were some cooking pots and some staples.

She looked in his sack and laughed.

"At least we won't starve for a day or two. Were you planning a long ride?"

"Planned, didn't work out."

"Fire?" Spur asked.

"Nobody will be hunting us tonight, so why not have a fire and we can cook up something."

An hour later they had eaten bacon and cheese sandwiches and had coffee and then a can of peaches.

"Will you be going back north to Philadelphia?"

She sighed and stared at him frankly. "Yes. I'm convinced now that John is dead, but we'll never know for sure how or why. My mama would say come home before she loses another child. But I won't sneak out of town. I'll get the rest of my gear and ride down the main street and on to Springfield. No bunch of bastards like this is going to run me out!"

Spur chuckled. "Lots of grit, I like that." He sobered. "But dead grit doesn't help a body much. Remember that."

She leaned back and watched him in the soft lamp light.

"You are interesting. You treat me just like I was white. I mean you aren't put off, or embarrassed or upset. Strange."

"Not so strange. You're a person, a lady, a pretty lady, and I have always liked pretty ladies."

"But I'm black, a Negro."

He caught her hand and rubbed it with his. "None of the white rubs off on the black, and none of the black rubs off on the white."

Edith laughed. "You are a smart man, and wise, and . . . kind." She looked up at him. "This doesn't embarrass you, being here with me, spending the night here?"

"No. Does it embarrass you, bother you? I can take my bedroll out under the pines. I've slept out as much as in lately."

"For goodness sakes, no!" She smiled softly. "Now why would I let the best looking man I've seen in months sleep outside?"

"Just a thought."

"I haven't thanked you for saving my skin back there. Seems to me like this would be a good time."

She had been sitting by the small fire. Now she stood and walked over where he sat in the cabin's one straight chair. Edith bent and kissed his lips. She watched him.

"Does that bother you?"

"Yes. But I'm not sure why. Try it again."

She smiled and kissed him. Spur pulled her onto his lap, and kissed her back. He eased away from her.

"Bother me? Excites me is a better word. Let's try that again." The kiss continued, and slowly she opened her lips so his tongue could bore in.

His hand found one of her breasts through the blouse and she murmured softly. His lips came away and he kissed her eyes.

"Edith, you don't have to do this."

She smiled. "You don't have to either, but I don't want to stop anything we have started, do you?"

He kissed her again, then opened the buttons on her blouse. His hand crept inside and cupped one of her generous breasts.

"Absolutely beautiful!" he said.

"That feels so good!" Edith purred. She unbuttoned his leather vest, then his shirt and played with the black hair on his chest. "You feel so good!"

His hand caressed the mound, teased the standing tall nipple and he felt it grow hotter by the moment.

"Will you be cold?" he asked.

"I'm getting warmer by the second!"

He pushed the blouse off her shoulders and let it fall. Her twin mounds swayed a moment, then thrust out, still pointed and firm.

"Please," she said.

Spur caught both of her breasts, massaging them, fondling them until Edith moaned in pleasure.

"They like to be kissed," she whispered to him.

Spur carried her to the first bunk where she had spread out her bedroom. He sat her on the edge and went to his knees, his mouth closing around the softly dark breast.

He kissed them and licked one nipple and suddenly she climaxed.

"Oh, Lord!" she shouted. "I'm coming! Oh, Lord but it's a good one! Oh, Lord!" She fell back on the bunk, her legs spread and her slender hips pounded upward a dozen times as the sudden vibrations shook her in a series of spasms.

Edith wailed long and loud as the tremors blasted through her. She pulled his head down on her breasts again and went into a second series of long moans and yelps as she thundered through a second climax.

When she finished at last, she lay there a moment gasping for breath. Then she looked at him.

"Spur, tear these pants off me right now!"

He found the buttons down the fly and pulled the man's pants off her shapely legs. Before he could help she had pushed down soft cotton underpants and lay on the bed in the half light bare and delightful.

She sat up and began undressing him. His vest and shirt went first, and all the time she was telling him about the first time she ever made love. She was fourteen and had managed to stay a virgin that long.

Edith pulled down Spur's pants and saw the big bulge in his cotton, short underwear.

"Oh, Lordy!" she yelped. Edith ripped off his pants, then snuggled down to the top of his underwear and began to kiss them downward.

"Wonderful!" she raptured as she came to the forest of dark pubic hair. Then when she jerked the cloth down and his long, hard weapon raised she screeched in delight.

She caught his penis and kissed it a dozen times, then slid it in her mouth and pumped back and forth a dozen times. Spur was about to stop her when she pulled away.

"Quick, Spur! Right now! I've never had a white cock in me and I want you so bad!" She rolled on the bunk and spread her legs wide and lifted her knees.

Spur kicked off his shorts and went over her.

"Positive?" he asked.

"Yes, damnit! Hurry up or I'll get a butcher knife and go after you!"

Spur grinned and lowered. She gasped and helped and then her juices flowed and she moved and at once he rammed into her until their pelvic bones crashed.

"Oh, damn! Oh damn! Oh damn!" Edith screeched. "Marvelous! Wonderful. So beautiful!" She pushed upward so she could whisper.

"Handsome, sexy, Spur McCoy. Please fuck me hard. Fast and hard and then next time we'll do it the way you like. Hard and fast and don't stop!"

Spur kissed her and followed directions. He had never made love to such a thrashing, moving, jolting, responsive woman in his life. She was moving against him, then with him, and squirming on the hard bunk until he had trouble following her. Then she stopped moving and screamed so loud he was sure they would hear her in Branson.

He climaxed and her scream caught in her throat and she launched a series of spasms that made her solo action pale into a beginner's effort. They thrashed and pounded and wailed together as both finished their climaxes at almost the same time.

Spur fell heavily on top of her, then lifted up on his

elbows and knees, but she pulled him down and wrapped her arms around his back.

They lay there for fifteen minutes getting their strength back. Slowly she began to kiss his face. He roused and pushed up. They sat side by side on the bunk.

She looked at him and lifted her brows. "Lordy, I just never would have *dreamed* that we would make love. So *wonderful!* Now, I need to go outside for a minute, then I want something to eat. It always makes me hungry. I may eat up all of your food before the night is over." She kissed him.

'Hey, three, maybe four more times?"

Spur caught both her breasts and fondled them. "Edith, just as long as my strength holds out," he said.

When she came back, they ate cheese and some crackers she had brought.

"I should have some cold beer for you," she said. "Water will have to do, or coffee."

She told him about growing up in Philadelphia.

"Before the war I was just little. I didn't understand much of what happened. I was fourteen when the war ended. I knew we were different from the other folks. But I went to school with the other kids, almost all white. They tried to make friends with me because I was black, and that was the thing to do during the war."

"Then I started to get urges I didn't understand." She laughed softly and played a moment with his flaccid genitals. "This good looking white boy I knew told me he was having the same feelings and offered a try and figure them out."

Edith laughed again. "Boy was I dumb. He helped me figure them out all right. We went behind this big billboard on the way home from school one afternoon. He kissed me and I almost fell over. Then he got his hands on my breasts and I did fall over and he knew exactly what to do make me understand all of those strange physical urgings I had. Three times he showed me all about it that afternoon."

Spur finishd his coffee and picked her up. "I think it's time that you explain some of those urges to me. If you have time."

Edith smiled and kissed him. "Seems to me that we have the rest of the night. I'll try to explain those urges just the best way that I can."

# 7

The next morning, Spur rode into town the long way, coming around from the north. Edith had assured him that she would be fine in the daylight, and not to worry. She would go to town get her things together and say goodbye to her new found friends then ride out of Branson for good.

They had cooked breakfast and put the food things in a box. She had assured him that everything would be safe there. Nobody would bother it even if someone stopped by to use the cabin.

Spur watched both sides of Main Street as he rode along. There were few people around at seven that morning. He stopped by at the Branson General Store to get some cleaning oil for his pistol and some store bought patches. The tall, thin man who waited on him had a lisp, and Spur wondered if he was one of those who had hung Phillip Russell.

Out on the street, Spur left his horse in front of the store and ambled toward the county sheriff's office. He wanted to have a good talk with the man. There might be some way he could put the fear of the U.S. Government into him. There was little to lose here now.

If Edith were right, the Bald Knobbers would be after his hide sooner or later anyway.

Spur had gone half a block when he felt a change come over the place. It was nothing he could touch or identify. Two men lounged against the outside of a saloon a dozen yards ahead of him. A horseman rode slowly up the street. A farm wagon pulled in at the doctor's office behind him.

Then he knew what it was.

The silence.

Nobody was talking. There were no kids on the street, no women. He slowed and looked around as casually as he could with the hairs on the nape of his neck standing up.

A shotgun roared a dozen feet from him. His head snapped around in that direction and he saw the weapon aimed at the sky, but two more scatterguns pointed directly at his chest.

Sheriff Parcheck grinned from behind the just fired Greener.

"Just so there's no mistake, son, you're under arrest for the murder of Phillip Russell. Lift your hands or get two dozen double ought buck through your belly."

"Sheriff, you know that charge is a lie, why are you doing their dirty work?"

"Doing whose work, deadman?"

"You know who, the Bald Knobbers, the vigilantes who are bleeding this county dry and filling their own pockets."

The rifle butt swung from behind him and he had only a flash of it from the side of his eye before the steel plate thundered into his kidney and he went down in a sprawling, gagging, retching mass.

Somebody pulled the six-gun from Spur's holster and the derringer from inside his shirt.

Sheriff Parcheck stood over him looking down. A bucket of water from the horse trough splashed over his head and torso. Spur gasped in surprise and shook, and them vomited again in the street, not able to lift his face from the remains of his breakfast mixed with green bileish pleghm.

"Now, stranger," Parcheck growled. "You was saying something about our fair county here?"

Somebody grabbed his hair and dragged him to a sitting position.

"You got some complaint about how we run things here, McCoy?" Parcheck asked.

Before Spur could answer another bucket of water hit him in the face and chest almost toppling him over. He sat there, gasping for breath as the pain of the kidney blow slowly faded.

"Get him on his feet and bring him down to the jail," Parcheck said.

Spur let them drag him to his feet, then swung out with both fists, flooring one of the men and jolting the second one back a yard and a half.

A shotgun blasted from six feet behind him, aimed at the sky again. Then the gun butt slammed into the back of his head and Spur McCoy fell forward into the dirt and horse droppings on the street. This time he passed out before he hit the ground.

He came back to consciousness in jail, draped over a plank bunk fastened to the side of the steel cell with iron bars. He blinked, trying to remember. When he did he closed his eyes. No sense letting them know he was awake. He listened for five minutes, but could hear nothing. He was alone, and no one was in the other cells.

Slowly he lifted his arms, then pushed himself up until he sat against the wall. His head pounded like a thousand Apaches on the warpath. Gradually the din faded and only a growing throbbing pain slammed through his head. He could live with one pain.

The jail was the usual; steel bars and thick metal straps to form a steel cell. The door was six feet high and had a heavy lock on the outside and a chain and padlock for double precaution.

Somebody unlocked a metal door down the hall, came in and stared at him a moment, then retreated and a few minutes later, Sheriff Parcheck walked in and laughed.

"Well, our big hero doesn't look so goddamned good right now. Soaked, vomit all over him, muddy, hair all mussed, no gun and no hat. Damn what a shame."

Spur looked the other way, ignoring the lawman.

"I'm talking to you, badass!" Parcheck thundered.

Spur stood up, went to the bars that connected his cell to the one next to it and urinated through the openings.

"Stop that!" Parcheck roared.

Spur went back to the bench and lay down, never looking at the sheriff. The lawman began to rattle the lock, then stopped.

"Oh, you would love to have me come inside, wouldn't you, bit shot? Well, I ain't gonna. Not at all. Fact is we got a trial set for you in just about three hours. You was passed out for some time. Near ten in the A.M. right now. Come one in the afternoon, we hold trial for you.

"The Honorable Judge Abe Conners, presiding."

Parcheck watched him for a minute. "What's that? You say you want a lawyer. Well now, that is a pity. You done hung the only lawyer in town, outside of Nells. Old Nells went into Springfield about three days ago to buy himself a new suit. Won't be back for a few more days. He always spends a week at this little whore house on Ozark street."

Spur concentrated on taking long, even breaths. He was powering his body back into full strength if he ever had a chance to use it. The sheriff kept talking.

"So . . . we'll have the trial. The judge has decided because of the delicate nature of the charges, you will be tried without a jury. The public will be limited in the courtroom for the protection of the accused. The dead man was well liked around town." Sheriff Parcheck laughed long and loud. Then he turned.

"Well, looks like the accused won't have much to say in his own defense. Fine with me. Makes for a quicker trial that way. You'all have a nice sleep now, 'fore the trial. You got most of a day left. We never have hangings in the afternoon. Always sunup round these parts."

The sheriff chuckled as he walked down the hall, the sawed-off shotgun in his hands eased the triggers back down from full cock.

Spur watched his back as Parcheck went down the hall. Time! He didn't have a lot of it left. They would do exactly as the puppet sheriff said they would. Trial, sentencing and hanging in less than twenty four hours. He eased to his feet and found he could walk. Spur did some running in place.

His body was rested and recovered from the two

murderous blows. Now, how in hell could he get out of here?

He tried the four sides of the cell. All were sound and secure. The door lock was old, but adequate. He did not even have any wire to fashion a devise to pick it. The chain and padlock ended that hope. The ceiling was ten feet above. It was open beams made of solid oak. The raw sheeting over the beams looked an inch thick. No chance there.

Spur sat down on the bunk. He would have to make a move when they came to take him to the trial. A belly full of shotgun pellets was better than stretching a vigilante rope. At least it would be quick.

For the first time since he had been in the Secret Service, Spur feared for his life. He could very well be dead within eighteen hours. There had to be some way to slow down those bastards, but how?

An hour later he was still trying to figure it out. If there was a way, he couldn't find it. Parcheck and his band of killers had used this method before. They had worked out all the problems and perfected it. This gave them more satisfaction than simply shooting him down in the street. They gave the town the show of a trial and a real law and order hanging.

The door squeaked and keys jangled down the hallway. The voices came softly at first, then stronger. One was a woman's.

"Yes, I know he's the man you say killed Phillip, but he was kind to me. At least we owe him a last meal before the trial. I fixed it myself. Roast chicken, mashed potatoes and gravy, muffins, peas and lima beans and a cherry pie from my own tree. Now you can't deny a condemned man a last meal."

Spur listened closer. The voice had to be Priscilla Russell!

"Hell, all right," the sheriff's voice said. "But Archie, you go along and watch her every minute. Anything happens and it's your balls in the fire. You hear, Archie?"

"Yep. I hear, Sheriff."

Spur was standing at the back of the cell when he saw Priscilla and a guard come down the narrow way between the cells. She looked concerned, but smiled when she saw him.

"Mr. McCoy! Oh, thank God you're not wounded. I heard about you being arrested and I wanted you to have a good meal. Even a killer has a right to that." She was in front of the guard and now winked at Spur.

"Yes, ma'am," Spur said softly.

"Feed him, don't jaw at him," the guard growled.

She passed the covered plate through the narrow hole in the bars for that purpose. Then turned and showed the guard the dull silver knife and a fork.

"The weapons, Archie. Be hard for him to hurt himself with these, right?"

Archie looked at them, nodded and she turned and handed them to Spur. As she did she adjusted the shawl she wore over her dress. She let it come open at her throat and then reached down and unbuttoned two of the fasteners on her dress top so both sides of her breasts showed.

She smiled at Spur then turned back to the guard. She was in front of him so he could not see the prisoner. As she faced Archie she bent forward slightly so her breasts bulged out even more. She put one hand on her stomach.

"Oh, dear. Archie, I forgot the coffee. Shall I go out and get it?"

As she said it her left hand darted behind her back. She lifted the back of her skirt to her waist showing her legs and white drawers. Spur stared in amazement. Then on the back of one leg he saw that she had tied a four inch hunting knife.

Spur edged forward, slipped the knife from the string and touched her back, then he slid the knife inside his shirt. At once he sat on the bench and began eating.

The food was good, he ate all of it as Archie talked to Priscilla. She had straightened up, but let Archie take a good look at the pure white mounds of the sides of her breasts.

She had moved to the side, so Archie could watch both of them. She had decided she didn't need to get the coffee, and talked of the weather and horses with Archie while Spur ate.

"Hurry it up in there," the sheriff bellowed from down the hall.

Spur stood, held out the plate with the knife and fork on it in plain sight.

Archie stepped forward, scowled at Spur, saw that the tools were both there and took the plate from him at the pass through slot.

Priscilla turned to Spur. "Mr. McCoy, I don't think you hurt my husband, and I wanted you to have a good meal. No, no, your thanks are not needed. May God have mercy on your soul."

Spur knew she was putting on an act for the guard, but it gave him a jolt as he realized without the knife she brought he could well be hearing those words as the last of his life just before the trap dropped and he plunged to the end of a half inch of hemp.

Twenty minutes later Spur began to scream. He yelled as loud as he could and a moment later,

Archie rushed down the hallway.

Spur saw him coming and writhed on the bunk.

"Poison! She poisoned me! The bitch gave me poisoned food!" Spur screamed the words as loud as he could.

Archie came to the cell door and scowled. He was confused. He looked at the cell door, then down the hallway.

"Get me the doctor!" Spur croaked as if his voice were going. "Now! I can't live another hour without some medicine!"

Archie ran back to the office. Spur kept screeching. Archie came back a minute later.

"Sheriff is gone. I can't let you out. I'll go get the doc."

"No time!" Spur whispered. "Not much time for me." He slumped against the cell wall.

"Shit!" Archie said. He fumbled at his belt for a key and opened the padlock on the chain. Then he worked on the big heavy door lock and a moment later it creaked and the door swung open.

Archie had his six-gun out as he came into the cell.

"Now, don't move. I'll help you stand up. Can you get up a little?"

Spur had taken the knife from his shirt and gripped it in his right hand which he had slid behind him so the guard would come up his left side.

"No funny stuff, McCoy, or I'll shoot you dead. You savvy?"

"God yes! Get me to the doc. Fast!" It came out as a wheeze that even Spur had a hard time understanding.

Archie wiped sweat off his forehead. He looked out the door, then moved closer to Spur. He tried to lift him with his left hand and arm, but Spur let his weight sag. Archie spat out a string of obscenities and holstered his six-gun. He put both arms around Spur's chest and lifted him to a standing position.

As Spur came erect, he swung his right arm around and drove the four inch blade of the heavy hunting knife into Archie's back, and ripped it out.

Spur kneed Archie in the crotch and when he doubled over Spur brought his knee up again under his chin and snapped his head back, breaking his neck and killing him instantly. Spur grabbed the dead man's keys and six-gun and edged out of the cell. There was a back door, but it was locked. He sorted through the keys, found the right one and unlocked the door.

A quick look outside showed that the alley was deserted. Spur eased out, pushed the six-gun in his belt and put the knife inside his shirt. He walked away from the center of town, toward the small church.

No one seemed to pay any attention to a dirty, bedraggled man walking down the alley. He crossed the street, jogged slowly along the next block and came up six houses from the church. Two houses past it he found the alley and ran down it to the back door of the second house. This was where Priscilla Russell lived.

Spur didn't have to go inside. She had waited for him behind the house with two saddled horses and a sack of food.

She was wearing sensible riding clothes, a heavy split skirt and a hat. She tossed him a blue cotton flannel shirt to put on and an old hat.

"Mount up, they'll be coming any time. The shirt and hat might throw them off our scent."

Spur stepped up on the horse and they rode due

east, away from the middle of town, through a pasture, around a fence, and then into a thick forest of white oak.

When they were hidden, they stopped a moment.

"I don't see how you did it!" Spur said. "That was the bravest, most ingenious plan I've ever heard of. I bet Archie never saw a thing after you bent toward him in there."

Priscilla smiled, but did not blush. "I told you I was tougher than I look. To let Archie have a peek at my titties is a small price for me to pay for saving your life. Now, we better ride like crazy again. I know where there's a cave that Phil and I found one day. It had a hidden entrance. Come on!"

The lady knew how to ride. Spur followed her as she lashed her mount through the timber and brush, down a creek bed, over a low ridge, up another canyon, over another ridge and at last reined in next to a thick woodsy growth not far from a small stream.

She got off her mount and walked forward toward the wall of brush. Slowly she parted the branches and then she and the horse were gone, passing directly through the screen. Spur followed her, found the spot and worked through the brush. There was an opening there that had been enlarged by hand.

A minute later he was inside a tall, airy cave. It had a stripe of sunshine coming in over the tops of the trees, but still camouflaged enough so it could not be seen from outside.

The cave was deep, fifty or sixty feet that he could see. They led the horses in the back and ground tied them. There was a small fire ring, two beds made of fresh pine boughs, and a sack of staples and cooking gear.

"I brought things up here the moment I heard you were jailed," Priscilla said. "I couldn't let them hang the only man in town who could help me."

Spur caught her hands. "Thank you, Priscilla. You have saved my life. There was no chance I could break out of there without help. I had decided to make a try at escaping when they took me to trial. That was about eight chances out of ten that I would be killed when I tried. I thank you again."

She reached up and threw her arms around him and hugged Spur tightly. She stepped back quickly, a little embarrassed.

"Pardon me, at home we always hugged a lot. We were taught that it wasn't bad to let your emotions show." She smiled. "I'm just so happy it worked. I usually don't lift up my skirts that way and I prayed that you would see the knife."

She began building a small fire in the fire ring. "Next we eat and keep up our strength. I have some homemade soup, lots of fresh baked bread and two jars of jam. The rest of that chicken is going to spoil if we don't eat it soon. Then we go outside and you teach me how to shoot the eye out of a buzzard at fifty yards."

Spur grinned. He was still trying to realize that he was free, and not under the heel of a deadly regime that had almost killed him. He laughed and helped with the fire.

"I pretended that you had poisoned me with the food. Archie believed me all the way. The food was good, but I can always use some more of that chicken."

She looked up at him slowly. "What . . . what happened to Archie?"

"Was he a friend of yours?"

"Not really. He usually works in the hardware

store. We bought some things from him. That's all."

"Archie has sold his last pound of nails."

"He's dead?" She asked.

"Yes."

"Good!" she said with sudden determination. "That makes one less of them to gloat over how cleverly they killed my husband."

When the fire had burned down to glowing coals, she put a pot on and warmed the soup and the roast chicken. They spread a cloth over the pine boughs for a table and ate their fill of the slabs of fresh bread, grape jam, chicken and soup.

They cleaned up the leftovers and went to the small creek to wash the pots and bring back drinking water. When those chores were done, she smiled at him and held out her hand. "Now, Spur McCoy, you are going to teach me to shoot."

"Why?"

"Why? You have to ask? I'm going to learn to shoot so I can kill the three men who lynched my husband. Why do you suppose I risked my life to get you out of that jail?"

Spur grinned. "I had wondered about that. You're going to have to do some convincing."

She glared a moment. "Spur, you saw him hanging there. You cut him down! You know he was guilty of nothing more than trying to do what was right. He was a wonderful, naive, crusading child in a forest of bastards. There was no way he could win.

"I'm different. I'm not an innocent. I know how to fight fire with fire, and a thundering .45 with another blasting .45. And I can do it. You owe me, Spur McCoy. You owe me your life! Is there any more convincing you need."

Spur McCoy shook his head. "I just wish we had a rifle. A rifle would be easier for you." She went to the trees the horses were tied at the back of the cave and brought out a Winchester repeating rifle. "Will this do, McCoy? I tried to think of everything. I'm a planner."

This time Spur laughed. "You win. Let's get started."

# 8

Spur started teaching Priscilla Russell how to shoot the rifle, the Winchester repeater.

"Have you ever fired a weapon before?" Spur asked.

"No. I used to be afraid of guns. Now I'm not."

"Good. You'll have nothing to unlearn. The first rule for you is to get a good solid base to lean the rifle on. Don't try to hold it without any support. Rest it on a fence, a tree limb, a buggy, anything even a big rock. Lying down is a good way to fire a rifle."

He found a gnarled white oak that had fallen over and rested the rifle on a chest high branch.

"Hold it, put the butt against your shoulder and your cheek against the stock. You've seen it done. There, that's the way. Now look through the rear sight. See the front sight? Center the front sight in the rear one. Now move the whole weapon to the target.

He went on giving her basic rifle instruction for an hour. It was over thirty minutes before he let her fire the first round. On her first shot she hit the leaf that he had pinned to a tree thirty yards away with his knife.

She missed the target the next four times.

"Squeeze the trigger, don't consciously pull it. When you do that you jerk it and the front of the rifle moves, spoiling your aim. Try squeezing your whole hand and the finger with it."

She did and hit the target the next five times in a row.

They moved to the six-gun.

"Heavy, isn't it?" she said.

Spur showed her how to hold it in both hands. She caught on quickly.

"How far away can I hit something," she asked.

Spur knew what she was asking.

"No more than five or six feet. With this weapon you get close and make sure." He scowled. "Of course then you have to watch the bullet slam into the man's chest, see his eyes go wild, hear the scream and then the gurgle as he starts to drown in his own blood, and then watch his face as he crumples and dies at your feet."

Priscilla's soft face turned hard, determined. "Good! I want to see one of them suffer the way my Phillip did. Now, where is my target?"

The first time she fired the pistol at a tree six feet away she missed the tree and the weapon flew out of her hand. Grimly she picked it up, asked if it was damaged and planted both feet wide, held tightly, cocked the hammer and then shot the tree dead center, and she did not drop the weapon.

After a dozen shots she said her wrists hurt and they went back in the cave.

She heated up the boiled coffee left over from lunch and they sipped the steaming mugs.

"You shouldn't do this, Priscilla. I shouldn't let you."

"Spur McCoy, you can't stop me, not unless you keep me tied up when you sleep. You said you were some kind of a lawman. Just figure that you're doing the county a favor by letting me get rid of three of the worst bastards we have."

"It's not right, Priscilla."

"Lots of things aren't right in this world, Spur. Was it right when they hung Phillip? Was it right when they chased that black girl down the street after they tore her blouse off? Was it right that they killed that man and burned down his house last month?

"Damn right none of it was right. I'm not a lawman, I don't have to worry about that. I can wipe out the three men who killed my husband and then go back to Springfield and try to pick up where I left off my life. Is that too much to ask?"

"Yes, Priscilla. I'm a United States Government Secret Service Agent. Nobody else in town knows that, don't tell anybody. That's why I can't let you do this."

Priscilla put down her tin coffee cup and walked over to the blanket covered mattress of pine boughs where Spur sat. She knelt in front of him.

"Spur, I guess it's up to me to convince you that I have a *right to enact judgment* on these three men." She reached in slowly and kissed him. Her lips moved on his and before he knew it his lips parted and her hot tongue darted inside.

Spur pulled away from her.

"That's cheating. That is not logical."

Priscilla shook her head. She smiled and the dimples came into her cheeks. She was so cute and perky and sexy right then that Spur could eat her without a spoon.

"Spur, that wasn't cheating at all. This is cheating." She unfastened the buttons on her blouse and in one quick motion took it off, then pulled off a tight fitting undergarment and knelt topless before him.

She had a small smile on her face. "Titties, that is cheating, and I don't mind at all. I've got good ones and now is the time to use them to help me. Go ahead, touch them, play with them. That's part of what I'm offering to convince you."

Spur couldn't help but grin. Her breasts were pure, soft white, redhead creamy white, with faint red areolas centered by pink nipples that were as large around as his finger and now standing tall and he was sure pulsing with hot blood.

"It can't change the facts, Priscilla. This is still something you shouldn't do. Besides, it could be dangerous for you."

"Kiss my titties, Spur. You know you want to. Go ahead. Don't make me do it all."

Spur sighed, reached for her breasts and fondled them. He would always be a breast man. Big, little, medium, swaying, sagging, he loved a good set of tits.

Priscilla bent forward and kissed him again, then kept moving and pushed Spur over on his back on the blankets. He laughed through the kiss a moment, then felt her hips pressing and grinding against his, and he worked her legs apart.

She moved her mouth and nibbled at his ear.

"Now, isn't that better? We can relax and enjoy each other, and you will have no choice but to let me go do what I have to do. Agreed?"

"You're seducing me, lady, not the other way."

She pouted a minute.

"True, but I'll take my chances." She took off his shirt, then the second shirt and smiled at his broad shoulders and muscled arms and torso.

"I like a man with some muscles on him. Is everything else as big on you?"

"Take a look," he said.

At once she unbuckled his belt, pulled down his pants and short underwear and his rock hard penis jolted upward.

"Oh my!" Her eyes were wide. "I've never seen . . . I mean I'm not used to one so big . . . Oh, my!"

They undressed completely and lay on the blanket. At once she rolled on top of him.

"Right now!" she said. "I want to ride you. Help me." She went over him and he assisted and soon she found the right spot and eased forward, impaling herself on his lance.

"Oh, glorious!" she yelped. "Marvelous! It's such a wonderful feeling, so . . . so . . ." Then she was busy, sliding forward and raring back and coming forward until she had worked out a rhythm that looked like she was riding a horse. Spur lay on his back enjoying the attention, then he felt his own steam rising.

Before he could move, she exploded over him. Her eyes shut tightly and she screamed, then she began to cry, but her hips slammed against him as she sought more and more of his staff. She banged against him and cried, then sobbed and pulled his hands up to her breasts.

She shook and vibrated with a long series of spasms, then came away from him and went on her hands and knees on the blanket. She looked over her shoulder.

"Please," she said. "Finish it this way."

Spur went on his knees behind her and she helped with one hand, then he drove forward and she groaned and yelped in delight.

"Now big Spur! Spur me all you can!"

Only a few moments later Spur lost his own control and he jolted his load deep inside her and they fell forward on the makeshift mattress.

Ten minutes later they had dressed and sat watching the fire.

"I'm going to go do it," Priscilla said, her red hair still damp from her perspiration.

"I guess that's your right, Priscilla. But be careful. These men are not the kind who will take kindly to being shot by the widow of one of their victims. Word will get around quickly."

She smiled and reached over and hugged him. "I knew you would come around to my way of thinking. I know where they live. Tonight would be a good time to start."

Priscilla stood and rummaged in a bag she had brought, took out a pair of pants. Without embarrassment she took off her skirt and pulled on the britches.

"I don't want to look like a woman when I'm out there. You realize I can't go back to my house. They will be watching it. The sheriff knows I brought the dinner, he'll figure that out fast that I helped you escape."

"Be careful."

"I will."

He caught her by the hand and turned her around and hugged her tightly. "No, you don't understand. These men are killers. They will fight back with deadly force. If you do manage to kill one of them, the other two will be on their guard. You have to plan each one carefully, then follow through as you have decided will be the safest."

She kissed his cheek. "Thank you for being concerned."

"I'd like to go along and back you up."

"But you can't. You took some kind of an oath. Don't worry, I'll kill them and fade away, probably St. Louis after this, or maybe Chicago."

Spur sipped the last of the coffee. It was nearly four in the afternoon.

"I'm going. I'll wait until darkness to go into town. It should work out fine."

"I might come into town, just stay in the background, an alley somewhere." He watched her.

Slowly she shook her head. "No, I wouldn't like that. You're in enough danger as it is. I have to do this by myself. Do you understand?"

Spur sighed and nodded. "I should tie you up right now and not let you go."

She laughed softly, kissed his lips and backed away. She had hid her rich red hair under a man's hat, wore pants and a shirt that concealed her breasts. She looked like a twelve or thirteen year old boy from a distance. She got her horse, pushed the rifle into the boot and led the mare out of the cave without looking back.

# 9

Josh Newcomb shook his head slowly as he stared at his wife. "I don't like it, Mary. They are going too damn far!" Josh stood five feet ten, had lots of curly black hair, a tough, strong body from manhandling fencing and posts and hardware most of his twenty eight years. His father had run this store before him.

He stood behind the counter and concentrated on each word.

"Abe is the one going too far. He's got the whole county tied up, and now he wants to squeeze everyone again. I don't know what he thinks he can do with the money, him with the gout so often and that bad heart."

Mary watched her husband. They had two kids home with a neighbor and Mary worked all day with him minding the Newcomb Hardware store. It was a living. Even with the dues they had to pay to the Bald Knobbers.

Josh ran his hands through his hair and scowled. "This killing is what is going to do us in. That young lawyer. That one scares me. No, I wasn't in on it, but Abe said it was bound to happen. Kid was asking too many questions. Should have run him out of town, tarred and feathered, the way we used to do."

"He would have come back," Mary said. "His kind of honest men always do."

"Damn! You're right. But now Abe had this newcomer Spur something arrested. Threw him in jail and all set to have a joke of a trial. But Spur escaped first and killed the deputy. Gonna be hell to pay at the meeting tonight. Abe is going to want him dead too."

"You could always turn in your hood," Mary said quietly. "You know I've never thought much of this way of running a city or a county."

"That kind of talk could get your husband killed, young lady. Stop it. We can think that way all we want, but we have to be careful saying it out loud." He looked around the store but it was empty. Josh wiped a line of sweat off his forehead.

"Even five years ago it wasn't so bad. Then Abe came into town and he really changed the whole scope of the group. We used to have church folks running things. Now it's Abe, saloon owner, gambling hall man and whoremonger."

"Maybe you can elect a new leader," Mary said.

Josh laughed. "We don't elect anybody. Nobody is called president or mayor or anything. The strongest men in the group call the shots and if somebody doesn't like it, he can speak up. Lately the ones who spoke up loudest are now out in the cemetery."

Mary came over and put her arms around him. Her brown eyes were narrow, worried.

"You be careful. I know we agreed you had to be one of them, but just be cautious. Another two years and we'll have enough saved to leave here and sell the store. I've dreamed so of living in St. Louis where my sister is."

Josh kissed his wife on the forehead. "Little Mary, don't you worry. Things will settle down again. First the lawyer, then that strange scene yesterday with the Negro woman, and now this Spur character breaking out of jail. Abe has never lost a man he set his mind on killing. Not before, at least."

Josh looked around the store, saw a man come in and sold him a new spade, then came back to where Mary stood unpacking some hand tools.

"I remember my daddy telling me about the 'group' as he used to call it. Most of it began right after the war, when there was almost no state government and none at all in some of the counties like ours. He said somebody had to hold things together and they did.

"But he said for a long time a man had to be a member of the church and a resident of the town to be on the group. That kept it fairly well in bounds. They were all high minded men, concerned with keeping out the riff-raff after the war, and building a fine community where they could raise their kids."

"I reckon even now Abe Conners would join the church if he had to," Mary said.

"Sure, but that wouldn't change him. He's a criminal himself. That's about the only thing to call him. An outlaw with the power of a whole county behind him."

Mary unwrapped a ten ounce hammer and marked the price on it.

"I saw them with the Negro woman yesterday. Ripped her blouse off and chased her across the street. They were offering her for sale, right there on the street. She looked half dead with fear. But she stood up to them. She sassed that Hirum Streib back right to his face," Mary looked away.

"Josh, I think those men would have ripped her skirt off and thrown her down and done it to her right there in the street if that man hadn't come out and helped her."

"And now both of them are targeted for the undertaker," Josh said. "I can't understand how it came to this. Sure, once in a while the boys used to get out of hand. Like that man from Springfield who came in and started that Oak sawmill. He turned out the best quarter sawed oak lumber I've ever seen.

"Lots better than the quarter sawed old Harry was turning out at his mill. So Harry talked the boys into burning down his mill and hooraying him and his family half way down to Springfield. That wasn't right, but we told them and said no more of that, and everyone obeyed."

"Josh, don't you go getting worked up. You just go to that meeting tonight and be there and don't say much and then you come home before they get into any trouble."

"Wish it was that simple, sweetheart. It ain't." Josh kicked the back of the counter where his money box was. He loved this store and this town. It was the Knobbers who were ruining it. They were taking everything for themselves—some of them.

"I thought the dues thing would break up the whole thing," Josh said.

"But it started off small, you said, like a dollar a month to buy some beer and have the meetings. Early on you said they bought some ingrates stage tickets out of town."

"That's the way it started. Now it's a mite higher. We paid twenty dollars last month, and Abe says the dues have to go up."

"Twenty dollars! That's half of what we make most months, Joshua! You never told me."

"Yep, I knew you would be upset. All the members say the dues are too high, but Abe just grins and says tough, he pays them too. You know they told that young lawyer his dues was fifty dollars a month."

"That's outlandish!"

"Some of us were trying to talk him into leaving town before Abe got his dander up. We didn't make it."

"Lawyer like him wouldn't take in more than ten, twelve, maybe fifteen dollars a month in a town like Branson," Mary said. She sat on the edge of a small chair behind the counter and her face was grim.

"Joshua Newcomb, I don't want you to talk this way at the meeting tonight. You just hold your tongue. Don't do nothing to get Abe and the other leaders angry at you." She went and put her arms around him and pushed close against him.

Josh looked down at her in surprise. "Hey, right here in public?"

She reached up and kissed his lips. "We're married, it's all right. Anyway, I'd kiss you even so. You're the only husband I've got."

He kissed her nose and laughed softly. "Hey, everything is going to be just fine. Don't worry. I know these guys, I know how they operate. I'll be careful."

Josh took a deep breath and checked the cash box. He took out ten dollars and put it in his pocket.

"They'll be asking for money again. Abe ends up with most of it I'm damn sure. He says most of it goes to Sheriff Parcheck for his twice a year trips to the state capitol where he spreads around money like it's water. Abe says that's what keeps the attorney general and the militia out of our county."

"Sheriff Parcheck is the kind of no good who could do that kind of dirty work," Mary said. She went back to unpacking the tools, chisels, files, screw drivers and two boxes of stove bolts.

An hour later, Josh pushed through the bat wing doors of the Cat's Claw saloon, bought a nickel beer from the apron and went through the door marked "Private" into the back room. A dozen men were already there. He waved at some, sat beside Hoss Wilton who ran the livery stable. He had been one of the early members who had been a good friend of Josh's father.

"Evening, Josh."

"Hi, Hoss. Keeping them nags of yours running?"

"Tolerable. What's going on here with the Russell hanging?" He said it softly so only Josh could hear.

"Careful, Hoss. There aren't enough of us left."

"Yeah. I know. Trying to figure out today how to turn this around. Need to export about six people."

"Including one saloon owner?"

"The first one."

Their voices were low, no one else heard or paid any attention. Most of them were talking about Archie, and how he died, and what the hell they were going to do about it!

"Find the bastard and skin him one inch of skin at a time with a good sharp butchering blade," a big man with red cheeks and red hair bellowed.

"Naw, too good for him. Let's make him cut his own balls off, and then slice his pecker off a half inch at a time while he watches!"

That plan got some vocal approval.

"Before that let's find him and that black bitch and strip them both on Main Street and make them give us a dog style fucking demonstration. Then we can cut them both up at the same time!"

Abe Conners walked in and everyone quieted. Abe rolled up to the front of the room where a small table stood beside a chair. He sat down and stared out at the men from small eyes, set close together.

"Men, we have two problems we need to take care of."

"Yeah, Abe, we been chawing on that," Hirum Streib said.

"Good. I've got some ideas too. This McCoy isn't in town. He was seen riding hard to the west. He might be long gone by now. Just in case I want two men to ride out and check that log cabin about three miles out where the niggers hide out sometime."

Two men lifted their hands. Abe nodded. "If you find McCoy and the Widow Russell out there, bring them both back, alive."

"Might sample that Widow Russell a mite, first," one of the men said.

"Don't matter you do, just so you bring them back alive," Abe snapped and waved them off. "Next problem is that nigger cunt who needs discipline. Anybody heard where she might be?"

"Blacktown," somebody said.

"You want to go down there at night and look for her?" another voice asked.

Abe looked around. "So we find her in the morning. We should be planning a deer shoot in the morning. Everyone with rifles and sidearms downtown by eight A.M."

He stared over the group that had grown to eighteen men. He knew each one of them. Most of them he could trust with his life. One or two were marginal, but they were watched and listened to.

"We still got two hours of daylight left," Abe

said. "I want two more men to ride north toward Springfield and then circle back west through the hills, and see if they can spot anyone, or smell out any smoke. I figure McCoy and the Russell cunt are on the way to Springfield, but the woman will slow him down, and they'll camp come dark."

Three men lifted hands. Abe waved at them all. "Remember, we want them alive, back here. Anything else is up to you."

The men left laughing and saying what they would do to Priscilla Russell when they found her.

"We have to hit this hard," Abe said. "This is a direct challenge to our control. We let this go unpunished, and it will be the first step to the end of our rule. Do we want that?"

"No!" the men shouted in chorus.

"Then we have to stick together and keep things running the way they are. We sent Parcheck up to Jefferson City last month with five thousand dollars to pass around. He did a good job. We have a firm commitment from the attorney general, and the Major General of the Militia swears he can't find his way past Springfield, if he ever gets called out by the governor."

The men whooped it up, laughing and chattering. Two dance hall girls came in with trays filled with mugs of beer. Both girls had stripped down until they were bare to the waist, their breasts rouged and painted.

"Hot damn, tits!" one man shouted.

"Look, but don't touch," Abe called. "At least not until the beer is gone off the trays!"

The mugs were picked up and eager hands reached in for a squeeze and a pat on the breasts. The girls laughed and giggled and at last flipped up their skirts to show off their fancy lace panties. Then they hurried out the door.

"You men know where the girls work, you get the urge," Abe said. "Members get into them pussies at half price!"

Again the man hooted and shouted and started calling out numbers about who would be first.

"Dues," Abe called to quiet the men. "This kind of operation takes money. We don't have a regular county assessor or county taxes, so we get our operating capital by collecting dues. Couple of the boys and me decided that everyone in town is going to pay taxes. Like in any county. I'll pick a man to list all the people and what they own and then set up taxes, fifteen, twenty dollars a family."

"Yeah, great idea," somebody called.

"Then our own dues won't be so much, right Abe? We do all the dirty work. Let the public pay for it."

"Great idea Hirum. Soon as we get our system working, the members here won't have to pay dues. Until then we need another ten dollars from everybody. I'll pass a hat around. Sure hope the total comes out even when I count. I trust you men."

"What about the Negro bitch?" a voice called. "What we going to do with her?"

Abe grinned. "You ever had any black meat, Willy? Hell, lots of things we can do with her. Soon as we catch her. Could have our own private bawdy house, just her and free servicing to members, no more than a dozen a night."

The men laughed and whooped in anticipation.

"Course she might object."

Laughter.

"We find her first."

"How did McCoy get out of jail?" Josh asked.

Abe looked sour. "Hell, I guess everybody'll know soon. We had him locked up tight, took him this morning with no problem. Trial set for this afternoon. Then that asshole Parcheck let the Russell woman in with a dish of food. He said he checked it, no way she hid anything in it.

"Course he didn't search her. He had Archie go along and watch her. Somehow she got a knife to McCoy without Archie seeing it. Don't know for sure, but she could have flashed some leg or maybe let one tit slip out of her dress. Old Archie would have been all eyeballs for her and not worried a shit about his prisoner. Course we'll never know for sure.

"Archie got back the plate and table knife and fork, and half hour later McCoy got Archie back to his cell somehow and knifed him and broke his neck and got away out the back door.

"Widow Russell is gone and so are both her horses, so we figure the two of them lit out somewhere."

As he talked, Abe Conners counted the money in the hat. Then he counted the men in the room including himself. He took a ten dollar greenback from his pocket and put it in the hat. "Yes, exactly right, men. We'll collect from the five who are gone soon as they get back. Anybody not have anything to do tonight, might mosey around town and the safe parts of blacktown and look for that nigger slut."

He looked around. "Anybody have any questions, or anything to say about our operation?"

Nobody said a word.

"Everybody gets another free beer at the bar, after that you're drinking on your own. Stay ready for some action. We got two projects in the works."

# 10

Priscilla Russell asked Spur again how she looked.

"Is my shirt loose enough so my breasts don't show?" she said not at all embarrassed.

"Yes, but it's a bad idea, you going to town. "These men are organized, they protect each other."

"Spur you men are always talking about 'things that a man has to do.' Well, this is one of those things that *I* have to do. I couldn't go on living in peace if I don't try to get them. All the rest of my life I would be scolding myself and telling myself what a lump I was.

"I have to settle this once and for all. Then I'll be able to sleep, I'll be able to get on with my life. Right now everything is on stop, until I have a short meeting with those three men. Can you understand that? Do you have any idea how empty I feel inside?"

"Yes. But as a lawman I should stop you. You're doing exactly what they are. Lowering yourself to their level. Is that what you want?"

"No, I want them dead. I hope you understand. I

know you won't try to stop me, and I thank you for that. When this is all over I'll come back and we can ride together on our way into Springfield."

She smiled, a bit of shyness glowing through. "I know my husband has been dead only a day, and I won't even be able to go to his burial, but when we were making love . . ." She closed her eyes. "Well, I hope you understand. I wouldn't mind another few days of being with you."

Priscilla turned, felt a flush on her cheeks as she mounted her horse and made sure the Winchester was in the boot and the big six-gun safe in her saddle bag.

Then she rode.

She knew the way and came to town just as dusk crept over the peaceful looking settlement. She tied her horse at the edge of town and carried the rifle over her shoulder the way she had seen boys do as they came back from hunting.

Lots of them did not bring back any game, so she did not feel out of place.

But she did feel strange. *She was going to kill a man, two or three if she could!* The full weight of it could not slash through her determination. She would cry for the men's widows later. Now was action time.

She knew where Barney Figuroa lived, about a block down from her own house. She wished she could go back there and get some more clothes and some of the food she had canned. But that was not possible. Sheriff Parcheck would have two men watching the place.

She found the spot she wanted after ten minutes of searching. The Figuroa house was near the end of the block. Directly across from it was a vacant home, with a doghouse that had been built alongside the residence. It was exactly the right height.

She could stand behind the doghouse, rest the rifle on the roof of the shelter and be ready for a shot. She hoped that Barney had not come home yet. If he had he might be leaving to go to a saloon or to a meeting of the Knobbers. She knew they met in Abe Conners' saloon. If she didn't find him coming home, she would march up to the house and knock on the front door and use the pistol.

Priscilla watied for what she guessed had been a half hour. Twice she moved and stretched and tried to relax. No one could see her. She had the rifle all ready to fire, the safety off. She heard voices and looked again.

Two shadowy shapes came down the street. One man was tall, the other medium height. They were talking, laughing, saying something about the bar wenches in the Cat's Claw. Then the words came clear as the men stopped in front of the Figuroa house.

"Barney, you are half drunk, you know that?" one man said. The taller of the two shook his head.

"No chance way, that I am drunk about by half as much," he said. Then he giggled. Both men roared in laughter.

"Soused to the top of your old eyeballs," the shorter man said.

Figuroa shook his head again and staggered a step away as he nearly lost his balance.

"Barney, think you can find your way from here to the front door?" the shorter one said.

Barney nodded. "After you leave," Barney said. "Shoo, scat, get the out of here. Hell!"

They both laughed again, then the shorter man waved and walked quickly down the street. Barney looked at the door and took two steps toward it, then he staggered off the sidewalk into the dry lawn. He snorted, got back on the walk and moved two more steps toward the door.

Priscilla sighted through the rifle at the shadow, waited until he got to the steps where he would pause. When he stopped and stared at the steps, she slowly squeezed her whole hand with the sights in the middle of Barney's back.

The rifle thundered and she worked the lever the way Spur had taught her to bring another round into the chamber. When she looked for Barney he was sprawled face down on the small porch. She aimed at the fallen figure and fired twice more, watching each slug slam into the fallen body. Then she put the rifle over her shoulder and walked past the vacant house, to the alley behind it, and down to the far end of the block.

She knew exactly where she was. It was four blocks to her horse, and there were only a scattering of houses between her and the animal. It was dark, she walked slowly, careful not to show any sign of nervousness.

A screen door banged behind her. A woman screamed. Lights flared in some of the houses on the same block the Figuroas lived on. Then she heard hoofbeats on the same street and she walked faster.

There would be no problem getting to her horse. Spur had told her the first man she shot would be easiest. After that the other two men would be on their guard.

Spur McCoy had let the woman ride out of sight, then he saddled his horse, and wished that he had kept the .44 he had taken from the jail guard.

Priscilla had both weapons, and he had none. He would have to take care of that problem when he got to town. His gear had been impounded by the sheriff when he was arrested. He was sure it had all been used and given away by now.

Spur rode hard until he could see Priscilla. He trailed her, staying out of sight, following far enough back so he could close the gap if she were attacked. He wasn't sure what he would do to help her since he had no weapons.

When he saw Priscilla tie her horse and move away on foot, Spur rode on to the alley behind Main Street and left his horse. He prowled that alley for two blocks, but found no drunk who would not mind giving up his six-gun.

He checked the stores and soon found the hardware store. The back door lock was not complicated and he had the lock open in two minutes. Inside Spur found a display of weapons and borrowed a handgun and a new Winchester rifle and shells for both. He also found where the dynamite was stored and took twenty sticks taped into four stick bundles with blasting caps fixed with three foot fuses pushed into each bomb.

Spur left a message on the counter noting his "purchases" and guaranteeing that he would pay for everything as soon as he recovered his funds. He signed Spur McCoy, and went back out the rear door locking it tightly.

Now with some weapons and his own homemade bombs, Spur felt much more like his old self. His job now was to watch and wait. He found a convenient spot in the alley in back of Main Street and settled in behind some packing crates to wile away the time until the town came alive.

It was a little after eight o'clock by his pocket Waterbury, when he heard three rifle shots not more than two or three blocks away. Spur did not run that direction. He was sure there would be plenty of Bald Knobbers there to confuse the problem.

He wanted to see what they would do next. Spur had concealed his identity as well as he could. He hadn't shaved for two days, he rubbed dirt on his face to darken it even more, and the old slouch hat came low over his eyes. The blue cotton shirt looked more like it would be worn by a logger than a cowboy.

He moved slowly up the alley to the street and watched from the shadows. Spur cached the rifle in the alley where he could find it and sauntered onto the boardwalk, then leaned against the General Store front.

Somebody came running past.

"What's going on?" Spur asked using his best southern drawl.

"Christ, somebody's been shot. Old Barney Figuroa somebody said. I'm going for Doc Gibson." The man hurried down the street toward the medical office.

She did it. Spur had wondered if she could pull the trigger when her sights were on a human being. Evidently she had. Now the Knobbers would really start to roar.

He saw six men walk out of the Cat's Claw and march down the street. They all had rifles and side-arms. Abe Conners led the army and he walked as a man possessed.

Abe Conners screamed. "When did it happen? Why didn't you tell me? How could Barney get gunned down that way? That shitty lawman McCoy wouldn't do it. Who? Who, damnit give me an idea just who did this?"

Abe stopped. "Yeah, yeah. From ambush, right, a woman's way of killing. That damned lawyer's wife, the little redhead with the good tits. Had to be her, what's her name . . . yeah, Priscilla. Let's go up to that house of hers and see if she sneaked back and what we can find."

A few minutes later, Abe led ten men into the Russell house. They lit lamps and looked through every part of the residence. Two men found a small strong box which they shot open. Less than a hundred dollars inside in gold. Abe took it.

"She's been here since we saw her last, damn sure about that," Abe snorted. "You men want anything here, help yourself. In about three minutes this place is going up in smoke. Scorch it right down to the dirt, that little barn out back, too. Burn the damn thing down! Then let's see her use anything else from here to hurt us!"

Men ran out of the house with furniture, clothes, and some canned goods. Then Abe nodded and lighted lamps were smashed against walls and curtains on both floors. The coal oil gushed with flames and in five minutes, the whole place was on fire.

The Bald Knobbers stood around and watched. One neighbor tried to get a bucket brigade going, but Abe told him it was too far gone already, just be a waste of time.

Abe waited until the fire was raging, then turned and stomped away with his Knobbers down Main Street to the ground floor office the lawyer had used. They shot the door open and stormed inside.

Here they found nothing they could use. They trashed the files and desk and pictures on the wall.

Abe was still furious.

"Burn it!" Abe bellowed.

"No!" Streib screeched. "It's my building for Christ's sakes. He just rented it."

Abe laughed. "Then drag everything into the street and burn the shit out there! But burn it!"

Abe marched up and down the street as he watched the desk, chairs, file cabinets, book racks and a dozen boxes of papers and books create a large bonfire in the middle of Main Street.

"Got to find her!" Abe kept screaming to anyone he came near. "yeah, house to house. Right now. Streib, Smith, I want you to deputize fifty men right now. Bring the damn sheriff. We're going to do a house to house search until we find that bastard of a woman!"

Smith rubbed his chin. "Think that might be going a little bit too far, Abe?"

"Damnit no!" Abe roared. He took out his six-gun and blasted five shots into the sky.

"All you men, gather round. I've got an announcement to make. Every man in this community is hereby pressed into service of the Taney County Sheriff's Office. You're all deputized. Now round up every man from the saloons and whore houses. Let's move, and keep that bonfire going to give us some light. I need at least seventy five men out here in ten minutes. So move it, NOW!"

Men scattered into the saloons, rousted drinkers and gamblers out. One man leaned out a second story window with his woman, then vanished and came running into the street still buttoning his fly.

In fifteen minutes, Abe Conners had every man awake in Branson standing in the middle of Main Street. He got to seventy, then stopped counting. The time was a little after eight P.M. and the weather was clear.

When everyone was there, Abe stood on a chair on the boardwalk in front of the freight office.

"Men, we've got a tough job to do. A woman

gunned down our friend and neighbor, Barney Figuroa tonight. Cold blood shot him three times from ambush."

There were outraged shouts and yells.

"We're looking for that woman. Her name is Priscilla Russell, a redheaded female about twenty-eight years old. We don't know where she is, but she's probably staying in one of the houses or barns or businesses.

"First we want you store owners to open up so we can look through them, then we'll get to the houses. We're gonna search every building in town and then head for blacktown as soon as it gets light if we need to.

"I figure we'll find her here. So let's get moving. We don't aim to hurt no one, but explain to the good folks of Branson it's for their own good. We got to find ourselves this vicious killer before she gets around to you and me!"

With a whoop the men scattered. There was no direction, no order. It was simply a small army of men working down Main Street poking through every store and business, then swinging half of the men to each side of Main and working down the strings of houses on First and Second streets.

The merchants all cooperated. One man was out of town so Abe was called and they shot his door open, searched the small store and padlocked it so no one else could get in.

A widow on First Street behind Main objected to three men coming into her house. Abe ran to the house, explained patiently to the woman and at last she said the men could search, as long as Abe stood there and waited for them. He did.

The search progressed for an hour. Most of the houses had been checked out, some of them twice.

Down on the far corner of Second Street Vern Smith came up with a prize.

He walked up Main to the fire where Abe had been most of the night and showed off his find.

"Abe, look what we found down there on Second, one little black nigger girl just mad as hell."

Abe turned and saw Edith Washington, the Negro who had given Streib such a bad time the day before.

"Well, well, well. Looks like we caught one fish in our net. Not the big one we wanted, but a little one who needs a few lessons in how to be a nigger in Branson."

Abe walked up to Edith and grabbed the top of the dress she wore and ripped it down the front to the waist. Quicker than he thought possible her hand lashed out at him, slapping him hard across the face.

Abe's reflexes took over and he punched her in the stomach, then his right fist hit the point of her pretty chin and she doubled over and fell into the dirt.

"Get her up, and strip her naked!" Abe roared.

Eager hands tore the dress and chemise off her, then ripped and cut off her white drawers that covered her down to her knees. Abe watched them and laughed.

"Now, high and mighty, northern nigger. We gonna show you where you belong." He pointed to two men. Stand her up and hold her arms and don't let go." The men sprang forward, grabbed her arms and held them out straight so she couldn't bite or kick them.

"You two, get her legs and spread them. You let her move and I'll kick your butts!"

Edith fumed and ranted at them, but she would

not cry. "You touch me anywhere else, and you'll all die!" Edith shouted. "Is this how Branson treats women?" She screeched it, and the men laughed.

"Me first," Abe said unbuttoning his pants. "Then as many of you as she can take. Understand any black cunt is good for at least fifty a night. If she gets too tired, lay her down on the boardwalk."

Abe walked up to face her.

Edith spit in his face and tried to bite him.

"Hold her fucking head and her mouth shut!" Abe thundered. "I don't want my nose bitten off."

One man held her from behind and pushed her body forward as Abe lifted his stiff penis toward her black crotch thatch and probed for the opening.

"Drive it in her, Abe!" somebody called.

"Men, I'll show you how we used to treat these nigger slave girls. Had me ten in one day once. Only two of 'em got knocked up!"

The men roared.

"Abe, we still looking for Priscilla?" Streib yelled.

"I can only fuck one at a time, Streib. Give me about ten minutes."

The crowd shouted and laughed and roared again.

Then Abe drove forward, lifted her buttocks to change her position and blasted into her vagina.

Edith screamed at the sudden pain, but the sound came out muffled behind the hand across her mouth. Abe grabbed her around the waist then and pounded into her. Soon his hands moved to her breasts at the last and he grunted and yelled in anticipation, then pumped hard eight times and stepped back suddenly pulling out of her.

"Damn, Abe. I thought you was hung better than that!" somebody yelled from the crowd. Everyone laughed again.

Abe got back on the chair he had used before.

"All right, now, this is a money raising event, new books for the school. Every man gets a shot at her, but it's two dollars a throw. Streib will collect, so just get in line all you big fuckers. We'll see how good you do in public!"

A laughing group of men quickly formed a line and began digging into their pockets. This was a shameful night all of them would never forget.

# 11

Spur McCoy had been dodging from building to building to stay out of the way during the search by the angry vigilantes. Once he joined a group of men going through a store then faded away when they left.

Now he came around a corner near the small hotel and saw the commotion down from the saloon. In the firelight he could make out the form of a naked woman. He ran forward and saw Abe Conners pull away from the nude black woman several men were holding upright. Abe made some remark and buttoned up his pants. Spur knew exactly what was happening.

He darted back to the alley, found the best possible spot and planted one of the bombs in a trash barrel and lit the fuse. It would burn for three minutes.

Spur raced two blocks toward the end of town, located the old barn he had seen and checked it quickly. There were no animals inside, just a stack of hay. Quickly he set the hay on fire, made sure it had a good start, then ran back the two blocks to the center of town. On the way he planted another bomb and lit the fuse.

He slid through the alley in back of the yahooing and yelling on Main Street, just as the first bomb went off with a roaring blast. The noise in the street stopped for a minute.

"Let's go see what that was!" a commanding voice bellowed.

Spur kept running away from them. A block the other side of the mass of men, he planted his last three bombs in spots where they would do no damage, but cause a lot of noise. Then he hurried back toward where he had tied his horse. He mounted and rode toward Main Street.

He could see the fire now in the night sky over some buildings. Spur hurried to where he had spotted the black girl being raped. She was Edith, he had seen enough of her twisted face to know that. There were only twenty men around her when he rode into the street.

Just then two more blasts went off on their three minute fuses, and all but three men dashed away from him toward the area the blasts had belched out fire and fury.

Spur brought up the Winchester and aimed carefully, fired and levered in another round and fired again. His first two bullets cut the legs out from two of the men who held Edith. She looked at him, scratched the other man holding her, pulled away from him and ran forward.

The third man grabbed at his six-gun and Spur put a round through his chest, knocking him down.

Spur rode up, reached down and grabbed Edith's arm and hoisted her onto the horse's back behind him. He drew his six-gun and sent two rounds at the wounded men, who screeched in anger and pain on the ground.

A man ran into the street directly in front of the horse. Spur shied the mount to the right. The man had out a six-gun and lifted it to fire. Spur had turned to the right and now the horse's head blocked his right handed aim for a shot. He struggled to get the weapon up in time to shoot around the mount.

The gunman stared at Spur and the naked woman. "My God!" he screeched. Josh Newcomb had a killing shot at either one of them. He lifted his weapon then aimed deliberately over Spur's head and fired two shots.

McCoy fired to the right of the man and spurred the mount and in a moment he was past the man who turned and fired high again. Spur frowned, wondering who the townsman was. Evidently he was not one of the Bald Knobbers or either he or Edith would be dead by now.

Spur charged out of town down a side street, away from where he had planted the bombs. The last one went off and he nodded grimly.

"Sorry I was late finding you, Edith," he said over his shoulder.

She had her arms around him and hugged him so she wouldn't fall off. All he heard were quiet sobs against his shoulders. They rode well out of town toward the cave. A mile away from the light of the barn fire, Spur stopped.

"Figure you're getting chilly," he said. He unbuttoned his outside shirt and took it off. Behind him Edith slipped it on, still without a word. "We have some extra clothes where we're going. Shouldn't take more than about twenty minutes to get there." Still she didn't reply and her quiet cry continued.

He turned to look at her, but Edith had her face averted.

"Edith, I'm sorry. I should have made you get out of town yesterday. Promise me you'll never go back into that place."

She bobbed her head and he angled the horse on toward the cave, furious at the men who had done this, knowing that he couldn't just ride away from Branson. Not after the killings, not after something as flagrant and obscene and terrible as this. Somehow a small measure of justice had to be done here, with or without the correct use of his badge.

Behind Spur, the Bald Knobbers gathered back at the remains of the fire. Some wood was thrown on and it blazed up.

"What the hell happened?" Josh asked the two wounded men.

"Six armed men jumped us!" One of them said. "Shot us up and killed Johnny and grabbed the girl and tore off. We was lucky to stay alive!"

"Six men?" Abe questioned. He looked at the second man.

"Damned if I know, Abe. All happened so fast, the explosion, then the fire, then somebody shooting at us. I went down and then she was gone and Johnny took a round right in the chest."

"Get Doc Gibson over here," Abe growled.

Abe looked around the group. "Anybody else see it?"

"I did," Josh said coming forward. "Wasn't six men, just one and he looked like that Spur McCoy guy you been talking about. My guess is he broke into my store, stole the dynamite and fuses and he set the barn on fire to get us moving around."

"One man! Damnit! You assholes!" Abe bellowed at the shot men on the ground. "Can't you do anything right? What the hell we got left to do now?" He stared around at the twenty men who were still there. "Lot of fucking help you bastards are!"

Abe walked around the fire, his hands clasped behind his back. He stopped and stared into the blazing oak two by fours.

"One damn thing certain, we track him first thing in the morning."

"Abe?" a small voice said.

At the second call, Abe looked up at Curt, one of the two town drunks.

"Yeah, Curt, you have a good time tonight?"

"Right, sure did. Also saw when Mr. Newcomb come running in from the alley and almost shot down the man who grabbed the girl."

Abe looked up, eyes alert, wary. "What did you see, Curt?" Abe asked softly.

"Well, heard the shooting, rifle it was, and I came out of the alley. Bottle was empty anyway. Then I see the girl being held by one man. He dropped her arm and grabbed at his hogsleg, then he got a round right in the chest and fell down."

"What happened then?"

"This big guy on a bay comes tearing in, grabs the girl, boosts her behind him and rides like crazy out east. Then Mr. Newcomb ran out of the street almost into him. Mr. Newcomb shot at the pair, missed. The guy shot back and then he was gone. Mr. Newcomb shot a couple more times, but by then they was out of range."

Abe grinned. "Thanks, Curt." He turned to Josh. "Seems you left something out, Newcomb."

"Nothing important. I should have shot him out of the saddle, I missed. That's it. By the time I got a second shot off, he was gone. I'm not a deadeye shot, not a practiced gunfighter like some of you boys are."

"Shoulda had him," the drunk said, shaking his head.

"Curt, if you saw it all so well, why in hell didn't you put a couple of rounds into him?" Josh said feeling ruffled.

"I ain't no good with a six-gun," Curt said.

"Neither am I, Curt."

Abe Conners stared at Newcomb for a minute, then looked back at the two men with gunshots. "Six men took you, did they, boys? You both got one hell of a lot of explaining to do." He kicked a stick back into the fire where the end had burned off.

"Hell, we ain't doing no good out here. Let's get some sleep and be back here at six A.M. so we can start tracking that pair. Every man bring two horses so we can gallop the whole damn way into Springfield, if we have to."

The men scattered, each going to his home. Abe kicked in the rest of the burned off sticks, swore a minute at the dead man, and decided to let him lay there until morning.

Ten minutes later, Abe was in his home, reaching onto a high shelf in his den for a special cigar box. Inside were neatly wrapped stacks of greenbacks. He added the hundred dollars from the strong box that had been in the Russell house and sat down and put his feet up thinking.

After she shot Barney Figuroa, Priscilla Russell had ridden into the countryside a half mile and waited. She could hear the shouts and occasional pistol shot in the town. When the explosions went off and the fire more than an hour later, she knew

Spur McCoy must be back in town.

There was nothing she could do to help him this time. She just wanted the commotion to die down so she could go back into Branson. There was no chance she could walk into Abe Conners' saloon and shoot him, so she had to get him at home. She figured he would be leading whatever hunt was on for her.

When the chase died down, she would be back in town and ready for him.

It was nearing eleven o'clock when she rode down the side streets of Branson. Everyone in town a week knew where Abe Conners lived. His was the biggest and best house in town, situated on a corner and set at an angle to both streets. The sidewalk came in right from the corner of the intersection.

Priscilla had stuffed her red hair back under the slouch hat, and pulled the shirt loose over her breasts. A boy. She still looked enough like a boy to pass, at least in the dark.

She rode straight to Abe's house and left her horse at a tie rail outside the decorative fence. There were still lights on in the house. She knocked hard on the door with the butt of her pistol hoping Abe would figure it was a man.

She reversed the gun, pulled back the hammer into full cock and held the weapon with both hands. When the door opened with the light on behind him, Priscilla could tell the man was Abe. She was in the shadows. She lowered the weapon and without a word fired a round through Abe Conner's belly.

Abe screamed and jolted back in the entrance way of the big house.

Priscilla stepped inside, saw the hatred and anger and pain on the man's face. But she never faltered.

"Abe Conners, you killed my husband, and a

dozen or so other men in this town. Now it's your turn to be dead." She raised the heavy weapon again.

"No!" he said. Blood dribbled down his chin from his mouth. "For God's sakes, don't shoot me again!"

"Just the same way you showed mercy to all those you have killed? The way you showed mercy before you hung my husband?"

A woman edged around a doorway staring at her. The woman's face was white with fear almost matching the color of her hair drawn into a bun at the back of her neck.

"Die, Abe Conners, the way you have killed so often." She fired three more shots as fast as she could aim and cock the pistol. All the rounds jolted into Abe's chest and he gurgled and died in seconds.

Priscilla turned, walked to the tie rack, got on her horse and rode away to the south. Mrs. Conners fell on her knees, screaming and wailing. It was five minutes before anyone came to investigate the shots at Abe Conners' house. His neighbors figured Abe was just disciplining one of his men.

His next door neighbor found Abe. By then everyone was drained, dead tired and most of the Bald Knobbers were sleeping. Three of his neighbors decided they would wait until morning before they tried to find the killers.

Mrs. Conners was hysterical. Neither the men nor their wives whom they soon called, could make sense out of her rantings.

Spur made one wrong turn in the darkness, backtracked until he came to the right small valley and rode up it to the cave. They went inside and Spur lit a lamp Priscilla had brought. He looked at the woman's things and found a bag filled with clothes.

"Edith, borrow something from here to wear. I'm sure Priscilla won't mind. All three of us are going to have to share a lot in the next few days."

Spur built up a small, warming fire as Edith picked some clothes from the bag and put them on. She came to him and gave him back his shirt.

He touched her shoulder.

"Edith, I'm sorry that I didn't get to that street a little bit sooner. I should have."

She shook her head slowly, then spoke for the first time since he had rescued her.

"No, Spur, you did remarkably well. I'd be dead before morning if you hadn't come. I've heard about men like these, but I never thought they could be real."

"So now you will go back to Philadelphia?"

"Oh, yes! Just as soon as we can ride out. What about food? I can go for two or three days without eating."

"No reason, we have plenty of trail food. This all began when I was tracking a gang of bank robbers."

"I heard, Sam Bass and his cutthroats."

"I lost them."

"But you saved me, twice now. I'm not giving Abe Conners a third chance."

They had sat down beside the fire when Spur had spread one of the blankets. She wore a blouse, a skirt and a jacket, and now hugged her knees up to her chest as she watched the fire.

"Edith, do you need to see a doctor? Did they . . . they hurt you?"

"Just my pride, that's wounded mightily. By body is not damaged." She flashed him a frown. "It wasn't like I was a virgin, was it?"

"You're probably the prettiest woman any of

those men ever touched."

"I want to forget about that. I want to go back home and tell Mama what I found out about my brother, and then get back to work."

"Work?" Spur asked.

"I'm a teacher. I teach fourth and fifth grade at a Negro school in South Philadelphia. Not even in the north do they let the races mix in the schools."

"That will take some time, I'm afraid," Spur said. He was quiet then, staring at the fire. He was trying to figure out what he could do that would be within the law, within his oath of office. There wasn't much.

He could go to the state capitol at Jefferson City and raise hell with the governor. But even that might not do any good. The Bald Knobbers undoubtedly had paid off some politicians somewhere to keep the state people and the militia out of the county.

What did that leave? A federal task force? The Army? Declare martial law? Hadn't been done since the war. You can't jail half the men in town. He scowled and pushed another small log on the fire.

"You're worried. Is it about the white lady, Priscilla?"

Spur shook his head. "No, I think she's quite good at taking care of herself."

"You must be a lawman, probably from the federal government. You must be frustrated because there is so little you can do here. Now you are a wanted man yourself."

"Exactly. If I go into town, I'll be shot dead or arrested by the Bald Knobbers. If I don't go in, they will continue to run roughshod over the whole county. I'm wrong either way."

Edith traced small circles in the sand beyond the

blanket. "I don't know if I can help you, but there's a story I always tell my students. It's about bad things happening. I say that sometimes it's like a rattlesnake. Most of my kids have never seen one, so I show them pictures.

"I explain carefully how poisonous the snakes are, and about the rattles and how the snakes strike. Then I draw a picture on the slate board and I suddenly erase the snake's head. I tell them that every time that the head of the rattlesnake is cut off, it ceases to be a danger to anyone."

Spur looked up and their eyes met. He thanked her a moment without saying a word or touching her. Then his face went grim again.

"Yes, you're right. If half the men in town had better leadership, they would go in that direction. There are only a few, maybe half a dozen in all who are the root cause of this whole problem."

He put another stick on the fire.

"Edith, how can I justify going into Branson and shooting down the six men who must be eliminated before the town can set itself straight again? I don't see any way that I can come near to convincing myself that such an act would be in the best interest of justice. If I killed them wouldn't that make me a Bald Knobber just like them? It means I'm taking the law into my own hands, the same way they are."

She watched him, then leaned in and kissed his cheek.

"Spur McCoy, you are a brave man, and a wise one. But twice I was caught in a street with a hundred rattlesnakes between me and freedom. And both times a brave man rode in and rescued me. The last time he had to kill one of the snakes to do it.

"Tonight there are three hundred people in that town, and most of them are just waiting to be rescued. A dozen at the most would move out and find some other place to rob, if Branson became a law abiding town. You know that, Spur McCoy."

"Then you are suggesting that I wade in there and wipe out half the Knobbers?"

"I can't give you that kind of advice, Spur. I only know what happened to me, and that one man died, and now I'm free."

Before he could answer Spur heard noises outside. He leaped to his feet, grabbed the revolver and slid toward the far side of the cave. His gun covered the form that walked through the forested opening. It was Priscilla Russell.

Spur relaxed, lowered the hogsleg.

"Glad it's you," Spur said.

Priscilla eyed his pistol.

"I'm glad it's me too, otherwise whoever I would have been could be dead right now." She looked around. "Company?"

"Priscilla, this is Edith Washington. She ran into trouble again tonight in Branson."

Edith stood and smiled at Priscilla. "I think I'm wearing some of your clothes. Abe Conners wanted mine so he took them, all of them."

"Edith, I'm sorry. You're welcome to anything you need." She looked around. "Where's the coffee?"

There wasn't any. She got the pot and started some boiling on the edge of the fire. Priscilla edged two stones into the coals so the pot would sit on them and not tip over.

Spur watched her. Priscilla's hand was steady as she set down the coffee pot.

"I'm sorry, Edith," Priscilla said. She paused. "I hope Spur got there in time."

"Almost. I'm still alive. I am grateful to you for the clothes."

Priscilla smiled. "We have enough for both of us until we get to Springfield. We can't have Spur getting all worked up all the time looking at naked females, can we?" For a moment her hand trembled, then she began to cry silently. She bowed her head and when it came up her eyes overflowed and she sobbed.

Spur sat down beside her and held her as she cried. "You did it then?" he asked.

She sobbed and nodded.

"Barney Figuroa, right?"

She looked up. Tears streaming down her face. "Yes, and Abe Conners. I shot him too. Right at the door of his house. He's dead for sure. I had to do it, Spur. I had to!" She sobbed again, clinging to Spur as if he were the last person in the world.

When the coffee boiled, Edith used a cloth and took the pot off the fire and poured out three cups. Priscilla sipped at the brew black and unsweetened. Slowly her sobbing tappered off and then stopped.

After five more minutes she told them about the two shootings. Edith stared at her wide-eyed.

"These bastards have been getting away with murder too long," Priscilla said. "Edith, I recognized the three men who invaded my home and dragged my husband off and hanged him, for no legal reason at all. He had simply asked too many questions." She caught a big gasp of breath and sipped the coffee.

"Tomorrow I'm going back to town for the other one. I don't care now if I never get to St. Louis. But I want the third man who hanged my husband, the banker, Vern Smith."

"Is he one of the leaders?" Edith asked.

"Yes, Abe, then Smith and probably Hirum Streib are the three top ones."

Edith nodded. "One of them is dead already. Their leadership is shaken. If the next two men were to be eliminated, do you think the Knobbers would survive in Branson?"

Priscilla wrinkled her brow. Her dimples vanished. Then she shook her head. "No, I don't think so. Those three are the top leaders."

"Just a thought," Edith said looking at Spur McCoy.

Spur fidgeted where he sat, put two more sticks on the fire and drank his coffee. He glanced at Edith, who only smiled and looked away.

Spur drained his cup and reached for more. It could be a long night for him before he decided what to do the next day. He had made up his mind about one thing. As a lawman he could not simply ride away from an outrageous illegal operation such as this.

The ticklish moral question he kept asking himself over and over again was what could he do about it, and still stay within the law?

# 12

Word of Abe Conners' killing rocketed through the small town at sunrise. By nine A.M. everyone in Branson knew that Abe had been shot down in his own doorway the night before.

The Knobbers had started gathering at dawn in Main Street, but when they heard about Abe's killing, they all went to the saloon he had owned and sat around in twos and threes talking quietly. There was an ugly desperation generating.

Vern Smith came by at seven-thirty and took over the small table where Abe had sat. No one else had moved toward the chair. It was done. He had inherited the leadership of the Bald Knobbers.

"We're going to get him!" Vern said so softly and with such hatred that some of the men in back did not understand Vern. "We're going to track down this damn Spur McCoy and blow him into little pieces, tear him apart, cut his balls off one at a time!"

The men shouted their approval. He looked around. "You guys we sent out last night on patrol, did you find anything, smell any smoke?"

"Caught some smoke smell about three miles out, but danged if we could find any fire. Wind whipped up and the way that little bit of smoke swirled through the trees, we could have been a mile or two off. Found not a damn thing, really."

"So McCoy did land and stay. Which means he'll be back. He's a hardhead, that one is. Anybody who could get away from Parcheck has to be. Think we can just take it for granted that he killed Abe. Figures. But how would he know where Abe lived? How would he know a lot of things?"

Vern looked around. His slight limp was no handicap now. He was talking, his long suit, and he could sway people.

"What I'm saying, is that I think it's time we cleaned house. I know that we have a traitor in our midst. We have a spy, someone who does not truly believe the way we do. Before we go after this Spur McCoy bastard, we must root out this traitor and put him on trial.

"We do it this morning, right now!"

The men looked around at each other. They were in the back room of the saloon, and only the hard core were there. There had been twenty men, but now they were down to eighteen, minus one who went to Springfield.

"Christ, Vern. You sure?" one man asked.

"Yes, I'm sure and it isn't you. How else could this McCoy know that both Abe and Barney were in on the execution of that young lawyer? How else would a stranger in town know where both the men lived?"

Vern looked around at the men. "Most of you have been active in our work lately. But three or four have not. Makes a man wonder." He stared from man to man. "Does anybody have any charges to make against one of our members about treason?"

There was no response.

"Then I'm going to ask some questions." He glanced at the men and his glance stopped at Josh Newcomb. "Josh, how long have you been in the Band of Twenty?"

"About four years now, Vern. Ever since I took over the store from Pa."

"Yes, that seems about right. Your father was a good man. As I remember, you haven't ridden with us often."

"I'm alone at the store most of the time, Vern, you know that."

"Yes. True. But most of our work is done after store hours. Is there some special reason you don't participate more?"

"I guess I'm not a violent man, Vern. I know we have to keep outlaws and gamblers and gunsharps out of town, and I support that."

"Are you saying, Josh, that some of our actions are not against these kind of troublemakers?"

"I think that is a fair statement, Vern."

"Then you don't agree with our basic principles, do you?"

"It depends on who tells them, I guess."

Vern motioned Josh to come forward. "Josh, come down here and let's talk this out."

Josh stood slowly, there was a faraway look in his eyes. He moved slowly, then stood in front of the small table. Vern did not stand.

"Josh, did you have a good shot at Spur McCoy last night when he rode past you?"

"Yes. But I'm no marksman with a pistol."

"You shot and you missed him from ten feet?"

"That's right."

"There has been some talk that you missed him on

purpose, that you disapproved of our fun time with the woman. Is that true?"

"Vern, is it true that you run our banker out of town because he was a better money manager than you are?" Josh asked in an even voice.

"Bastard!" Vern exploded. He jumped to his feet waving his arms. "That man was a cheat! He was foreclosing on property."

"Folks who knew said he was within the law, he was doing nothing that you haven't done over the years on bad debts. Vern, how can you accuse me of missing a shot with a .44 when you ran old Harvey out of town because he was hurting your business?"

"Enough! I am not on trial here." Vern's face was red, his heart pounding. He sat down and straightened his shoulders. "Josh Newcomb, you are hearby charged with being a traitor to the Group of Twenty, that you have not participated in our work, and that you deliberately failed to shoot Spur McCoy when you had no excuse to miss. Your trial will begin at once."

There was a chattering of voices.

"Vote" a voice said. "We always used to vote on things like this."

"No!" Vern thundered. "There will be no goddamned vote on this matter. The trial has begun. Is there anyone who wants to act as Josh's defense lawyer?" Nobody said a word.

"I'll act as my own defense," Josh said. "Not that it will make much difference. When Vern smells blood, there is little that can stop him. Where did you get such a blood urge, Vern? Was it when you rode with Quantrel? I heard that's how you got enough money to open a bank in the first place.

"Seems you looted this northern bank and turned

over about half of the gold to the Rebel treasury, the rest went into a hole in the ground that you came back for later on."

Vern jumped up and slammed his fist into Josh's belly, then his other into Josh's jaw. Josh jolted back a step.

"You never did have much power without a gun in your hand, Vern."

"Shut up! This court is now in session. I'm the first witness. Last night this man, Josh Newcomb, had a chance to kill Spur McCoy, but he deliberately missed the shot. That makes him a deadly traitor to the cause of the Group of Twenty. If Newcomb had killed the madman, McCoy, as was his duty, then Abe Conners would be alive right now, and we would not be having this meeting."

"Yeah, yeah!" someone shouted.

"Vern is absolutely right," Josh said. "Abe Conners was killed last night, only I didn't do it. I was home with my wife after our search and the fire ended. Abe was killed an hour later, I'm told. Your job is to find out who did the killing."

"Wives are not able to testify for their husbands," Vern said. "They use crotch logic and it never washes. What we need here are some more witnesses about Josh Newcomb. He's the one on trial."

Hirum Streib stood up. "Vern, I got something to say. I knew Josh's dad. The old man was all right, but fussy. He never really joined with us. He didn't oppose us, but he wasn't really one of the Twenty.

"Now as for Josh, I've been watching him. He ain't never dirtied his hands, know what I mean? He even went along a time or two, but no blood on his hands. If I didn't know better, I'd say he was a spy for somebody at Jefferson City. He's writing down names and places. Bet he has a diary of things he don't like around Branson. Far as I'm concerned, Josh is our traitor."

Josh stared at Streib for a minute. "Hirum you are an asshole!"

Somebody laughed. "Can't argue with that!" Somebody else said. Everyone roared.

"Hirum you were always an asshole, and you always will be an asshole," Josh thundered. "You wouldn't know an honest man if he rammed a pitchfork handle six feet up your dingus and it came out your mouth!"

The men roared again. Hirum had never been a favorite of the Group of Twenty.

"Enough of the name calling," Vern said sternly. "This is a court, let's maintain some order. Are there any more who wish to speak for or against the defendant?"

"Always been fair and honest with me," a man at the side said. He stood, and Vern waved at him.

"Hans, we're not concerned if he's fair or honest, is he a traitor to our cause? That's the question."

The man sat down.

Josh looked at Vern. "Face it Vern. You don't have any evidence at all that I did anything against the Group. You just think that I tried not to shoot a man. For that you're going to hang me?"

Vern grinned. "Now there is an idea. We ain't had a good public hanging in weeks. Looks like most of the evidence is in. Since I'm operating as the jury here, guess I should give my verdict."

He stood and marched back and forth twice. "I the jury do hereby find the defendant, one Josh Newcomb, guilty as charged."

There was a chorus of hurrah's. One or two of the men frowned deeply.

"Sentence is that the condemned by hanged by the neck until dead. Place will be the old black oak next to the hotel, high noon today. Any objections?"

There were none. Vern didn't think there would be any.

"Tie up the prisoner so he won't be tempted to run away. He's got another hour and a half to live."

One of the men bound Josh's hands in front of him and tied him to a chair. Nobody went near him. It was as if he had a plague and they would catch it.

Vern sent four men to follow Spur's tracks where he went out of town last night. "He's riding double, we know that, so try to find the deep set of prints and follow them till hell freezes over. Might look for that smoke again. I want one of the same men who was out yesterday to be along."

The team was formed and rode off. The men were cautioned not to tell anyone about the upcoming hanging. It would be a surprise. There was less chance for opposition that way.

Vern waved as the men left. "We want to make sure of this. I want three men with repeating rifles on roofs overlooking the hotel. Get in spots where you have a good field of fire. We don't want nobody spoiling this hanging. Rest of you scatter and keep your mouths shut until high noon."

In the hardware store, Mary waited on a man for some fencing, said he'd have to load it himself since Josh wasn't back yet. The man paid and said he could do that.

Mary looked down Main Street from the store's front door and saw some of the men she knew were Bald Knobbers coming out of the Cat's Claw. She frowned. Where was Josh? She decided that he would be along in a minute. She hummed as she went back to the counter. It had been a good morning.

She had sold two batches of fencing, and several other good sized orders. Maybe the day she could get away was coming closer and closer.

Where was Josh? She walked back to the front door as Hirum Streib sauntered by. He tipped his grimy hat and nodded at her, but he looked away quickly. She frowned. Hirum was not one of her friends, but she knew him, the way she knew almost everyone in town. A few people moved in each year, but they soon found their way into the hardware store.

Small towns were like that. She liked it here. But she was also excited about the thought of moving to St. Louis. The city would give the kids a chance to be somebody, to get a good schooling and learn things.

Another man came along the boardwalk and she knew he was with the Group. She called to him.

"Wilbur, did you see Josh? He should be back by now from the meeting."

Wilbur shook his head. "No ma'am, didn't see which way he went when we left. He . . . he should be along soon." Wilbur nodded and almost ran down the street.

Mary frowned and went back in the store to help a man find the size of stove bolts he needed.

Ten minutes before noon, Mary looked out the window again. Her stomach was drawn up so tight she could hardly breathe. It wasn't like Josh to stay away this long and not tell her what he was doing. Something was wrong.

Another man had come in for some binding twine, and he had hardly looked at her. He paid and left quickly. She wasn't sure but now that she considered it again, she was sure that the man was one of the Bald Knobbers.

She hated the name, she tried never even to think of it. Then she heard the first shots.

Men were at both ends of Main Street, walking toward each other. They fired their pistols in the air and then shouted. At first they were too far away to understand what they were saying. Then she heard.

"Big hanging at high noon! Oak tree at the hotel. Come one, come all! Big hanging at high noon!" The man closest to her took ten or twelve steps and fired his piece and shouted the words again.

Some people passed on the sidewalk and Mary called to them.

"Who is being hung?" she asked.

Two women and a man shrugged and moved on. Mary locked the front door and hurried down the street toward the small hotel and the big black oak that grew beside it. There had been hangings there before. She shivered.

"Who is getting hung?" she asked someone else. The man shook his head.

At the black oak, Mary saw that there was no scaffold. So it wasn't a legal hanging. A black mare stood there, with a bridal but no saddle. Mary cringed. It was to be a vigilante hanging! Well, she just wouldn't watch, but she had to know who it was.

There was not a chance that Josh was to be hung, she couldn't even consider that. Josh found something he needed to do. He would be at the store wondering why she had closed up in the middle of the day.

She saw Vern Smith and hurried up to him. He scowled when he saw her coming, but there was no way he could avoid her.

"Vern. Vern Smith. Just who is it who is being hung?"

"Nobody can say, Mrs. Newcomb. We all just wait and see."

"But isn't this . . . The Group. Surely you know."

He shook his head and turned away.

Mary stood there in the heat of the midday, staring at Vern, not even trying to swat a dozen flies that left horse droppings in the street and attacked her. A man looked at her, shook his head and turned away. She saw him but before she could get to him, he had vanished into the growing crowd.

Soon there were fifty people in front of the hotel. Five minutes later at noon there were over a hundred.

Vern Smith rode into the center of the crowd on a horse and lifted his hand. On the signal two men walked out of the front door of the Cat's Claw saloon, pushing a man ahead of them. He had his hands tied behind his back and his arms bound to his sides with a second rope.

The crowd saw it and hushed. When the trio was close enough somebody recognized him and the name slammed through the crowd.

"Newcomb!"

"It's Josh Newcomb they're hanging!"

"Josh! Josh! Josh!"

Mary heard it almost at once. She rushed past the others, ran as fast as she could toward the three men. She jolted into one of the men beside Josh who carried a rifle. The surprise and force of her charge bowled the man backwards until he lost his balance and fell.

Mary set upon the second guard, clawing at him with her fingers, tearing down the corner of one eye before he brought up the rifle and pushed her away. Josh stood there watching. His legs were tied together by a short rope so he couldn't kick anyone.

"No!" Mary screamed. Tears flowed down her face. "No, no, no! Josh has never done a bad thing in his life! NO!" Two men from the crowd rushed in and caught her from behind and held her, then on a signal from Vern Smith they marched her along behind her husband.

At the tree the same two men held her.

"Murderers!" Mary screamed. "Isn't there just one man in this town strong enough to stand up against the kill crazy Bald Knobbers? They are vicious animals. They're ruining our town. Do you want to live in fear of your life?"

Vern turned to her.

"Mrs. Newcomb, shut up."

"Bastard!" She screamed. "Vern White is a murdering bastard and I hope he rots in hell for it!"

A third man came up behind Mary and pressed his hand across her mouth so she couldn't talk.

Vern nodded. Two men boosted Josh Newcomb onto the horse so he sat facing its rump.

Mary squirmed against the men, then got the hand out of position enough so she could bite a finger.

"Murdering bastards! All you Knobbers are killers. Start on women and kids next why don't you!" The hand clapped back over her mouth, then a dirty kerchief replaced it and was tied tightly behind her head. Tears streamed down her face.

Two men on horses rode up and threw a half inch rope over the big, strong oak limb. The other end of the rope held a hangman's knot noose. One of the riders fitted the loop over Josh's head and cinched it up tight. The knot lay against the left side of his face.

The other man took the rope back to the tree trunk and tied it off as tight as he could.

"For crimes against the people of Taney county, Josh Newcomb has been sentenced to die by hanging." Vern said from his horse. "The execution will be carried out now."

Josh sat on the horse with his shoulders back. He looked at Mary.

"I love you, Mary! I talked back to Vern Smith! That was my only crime. He's crazy. Somebody should shoot him right now. He's the worst . . ."

Vern signalled to the man on the ground near the black horse. The man lifted a wooden handled whip with six long leather strands and lashed it across the black horse's rump.

The animal bellowed and jolted forward. Josh Newcomb slid off the back of the quarter horse and dropped a foot to take up the slack in the rope.

The crowd was deathly quiet for a moment. Josh's neck did not break. His eyes were wild with fear and fury. In the dead stillness the crowd could hear him gasping for breath as the half inch rope pressed aginst his throat, then crushed his windpipe and his legs thrashed and his body jolted and twisted as he slowly strangled to death.

Not a person spoke.

Not a soul moved.

The quietness came rushing at everyone's ears.

They could hear their own hearts beat.

Then the man at the end of the rope stopped moving. A man rode up and looked at Josh, lifted his eyelids, put his ear to Josh's chest.

"He's dead," the rider said.

"The body shall hang there twenty-four hours as a warning to all who try to violate the laws of Branson," Vern Smith said.

The crowd exhaled long held breath and drifted away. There was no shouting or talk. Everyone felt the same terrible, awesome wonder about death. What was it? Was there really a life after death? Or was it one long, dreamless sleep? Nothingness?

Mary Newcomb sagged in the hands of the men holding her. At last they let go of her and she fell into the inch think dust of the street. She sat there staring up at the body of her husband. But she she would not cry. She would not let them see her weep!

Not now. The time for crying was over. She knew what she had to do. Vern Smith would not let her live long if she stayed in town. She had to get her children, rent a wagon and load what she could from the house and the store. Then tonight in the dark she would slip out of town and drive as fast as she could for Springfield.

She had kin there who would protect her. They would hide her if they had to until she could get on a train to St. Louis. She was going there after all. Not the way she had hoped. There was nothing here now for her except death.

How she wished she had insisted a year ago that they leave this hell hole of a town!

Mary Newcomb lifted from the dirt and brushed off her skirts, then walked back to the store. It would be closed the rest of the day. She had certain things to get ready. She had to be prepared if Vern tried to come and bring her back. Quickly she worked getting two double barreled shotguns ready. She loaded both, took along twenty five more rounds. Slowly she worked with the unfamiliar dynamite sticks.

She remembered what Vern had taught her. She made two stick bombs, tied them together with string and pushed the dynamite caps into the powder, then put a six inch fuse on each one.

It was only the beginning of her preparations.

# 13

Doc Gibson knocked on the front door of the Newcomb Hardware store but there was no response. He went around to the back and knocked again. Slowly the door edged open. A six-gun muzzle poked through.

"Your name and your business!" a woman's voice snapped.

"Doc Gibson is the name, a little sympathy is my business."

The door swung open and Mary Newcomb caught Doc's hand and pulled him inside the back storage room of the store.

She closed and bolted the back door at once. Mary blinked back tears and then reached out for him and fell into his arms crying softly.

"Doc! I didn't think anybody would even look at me again in this town," she choked out through her sobs.

"The Knobbers need me here, Mary. Up to a point I do as I please. You're right, they all are bastards. Some day things will get straightened out here, but not for years." He looked at the boxes and bundles on the floor by the back door.

"Good, you're fixing to leave. Tonight will be the best time. I'll go get a wagon so nobody'll know it's for you. Right after dark I'll drive it past here, then we go to your place."

Mary wiped the tears away and leaned back from her friend of many years.

"I begged Josh not to speak out against them, but he felt he had to, I guess. Wish I was strong enough to take a shotgun and go blow Vern Smith's head off."

"A lot of us wish we were that strong, Mary. No, best you get out of town fast with your kids. What are they, about four and six or seven now?"

"Melissa is five and Josh Junior is almost eight."

"What can I do to help you here?"

"Nothing, Doc, thanks. I'm just near done. Next I go home. Oh, I won't be here for a funeral for Josh. Could you see that it's done proper? A marker and all. I'll send you money when I get situated."

"No trouble. I'll do it. And don't you dare send any money." He looked down at the two shotguns and the boxes of shells. Beside them was a cardboard box with the dynamite bombs ready to use. He picked up one of the bombs and looked at it.

"Yes, wanted to be sure they were set up right. You've got twenty seconds or so after you light the fuse before it blows up."

"Thanks, Doc."

"I'll have the wagon here at seven o'clock. You try to drive straight through to Springfield."

Mary let him out of the back door. First she thanked him with a tight hug and a kiss on the cheek. Doc was a widower and he appreciated a hug now and then. She looked around, then slipped out the back door and locked it.

Five minutes later she had walked down the alley behind her home and hurried in the back door. Her neighbor looked up from where she sat watching the kids and Mary knew she had been crying.

"You better go home, Celia," Mary said. "I don't want you to get in any trouble count of us. Come on now, I know, I know, but you best be thinking about yourself, too." Mary gave her a greenback dollar bill and the woman was still too upset to talk.

The children had heard the neighbors talking. They both came out of the parlor where they had been playing caroms on the big board with the gold rings.

"Is it true, Mama?" Josh Junior asked, his face stiff and ready to cry.

"Yes, Josh. Your daddy is gone, he's . . . he's died. We're moving out of town."

Melissa ran up and hugged her. "Why did Daddy leave?" she asked.

Josh Junior scowled at her.

"He had to go, he couldn't help it. We'll talk more. Now, both of you get boxes and put everything you want to take in them. Your clothes and toys. We're going to leave as soon as it gets dark, but don't tell anyone!"

Mary stood a moment in the kitchen where she had lived for almost ten years. So long! She rushed then, using two old suitcases and cardboard boxes and packed her clothes and all of the personal things she could find.

She sobbed as she passed up Josh's clothes. There wasn't time and there wasn't room. In a fury she threw things into the boxes that had folding tops, and tugged them to the back door closest to the alley.

The last box she packed was food. Josh Junior came and helped then. He was grim faced, brimming with questions, but he didn't ask them. She would have to explain sometime.

They had a good dinner, she wasn't sure when she could feed them again. Then she made sandwiches, enough to last them for two days, and put it all in a box.

The time rushed past. When she finished the sandwiches it was dark. She and Josh Jr. carried the boxes out the back door to the closest place to their house where a wagon could drive in the alley.

When they were done, she told the kids to stay inside the house and not let anyone in, then she hurried down to the store's back door.

Doc Gibson was waiting with a farm wagon with two foot sides on it, and pulled by a pair of plow horses that looked sturdy enough. He nodded and she unlocked the store. She lit a lamp, then took a piece of paper out of her reticule.

"What's this?" Doc asked as she gave it to him.

"Don't ask a bunch of fool questions, just sign it on the bottom line under my name and keep it."

"Why?"

"Because I don't want the Bald Knobbers to get the store and all the goods. I'm selling it all to you for $3,500. But you don't have to give me any money. This is a legal bill of sale, that not even Vern Smith can contest. It'll be safe with you."

Doc nodded. "And I'll get somebody to run the store for me and send every bit of profit to you. You give me your new address and a new name as soon as you get settled. Then the Knobbers won't know it's you."

"Don't have to do all that. But if it does make some profit, it sure would be helpful."

"Yes, now let me load these boxes."

Mary loaded as many as the doctor, and soon everything was on board. They fixed a seat near the front for some boxes, and Mary put the shotguns under a blanket so one pointed to each side of the wagon but were out of sight. She could reach both of them easily.

In back she put a short mattress for the kids to sit on.

Doc jumped up and drove as they went through two more alleys and then came up in back of her place. She went inside to get the kids and Doc Gibson tussled the home boxes into the wagon. He rearranged the mattress and had everything on board by the time the three came out of the house.

"Melissa, we're going on a long trip. You can play in back and sleep on the little bed. Won't that be fun?"

Melissa frowned, shrugged and climbed on the wagon.

Josh Junior was already on the makeshift seat holding the reins. Mary gave Doc Gibson a hug and kissed his cheek. "You take care of yourself now. Don't let the Knobbers hang you, too. I'll worry about you."

"Good. Feels fine to have a pretty woman worried about me. Now get out of here."

Doc said a small prayer for their safety as Mary Newcomb climbed into the wagon wearing sensible trousers and a work shirt. She picked up the reins and quietly headed out of town.

They drove all night down the rutted track of a trail like road to the north and Springfield. By midnight both of the children were sleeping, and the horses were getting tired. She cracked their backs with the reins and they plodded forward at maybe three miles an hour.

She knew that as soon as morning came, Vern would find out she had left town. Doc said he would put up a notice on the front door of the hardware stating that it was now his legal property and anyone interested in working the store as clerk and manager, should see him at once. There would be somebody, Mary was sure.

Now her job was to get as far from Branson as possible. If she got enough miles, perhaps the riders Vern would send after her would give up and go home. Perhaps.

She ate another sandwich. She wasn't hungry, but the action of eating gave her something to do and kept her awake. She was sure if she went to sleep the horses would stop.

Mary watched the Big Dipper. It was true that it did rotate around the North Star. Early on she had seen it low and to the right, maybe where the hands of a clock would be if it were four P.M.

She watched it now and saw that it was almost straight over the top of the North Star. She wasn't sure what time that would make it.

Mary finished the sandwich and drove on. The ruts bounced the whole load and Melissa rolled to the side of the small mattress. It woke up Josh Junior and he pushed her back on the softness without waking her.

"Thank you, Josh. You know you're going to have to be the man of the house now for a while."

He sat up rubbing his eyes. "Uh huh. I know. Want me to drive?"

Mary smiled in the darkness. "No, you can drive tomorrow while I sleep. Now, you get your rest. I'll need you tomorrow for sure."

Twice she went to sleep before daylight. The first time she fell to the side and woke up. Mary was not sure how long she had been sleeping. She looked up at the Big Dipper and found it lower to the left of the North Star. The horses stood stock still in the middle of the trail waiting, perhaps sleeping themselves, she was not sure.

Mary whacked them with the reins and they snorted and moved ahead grudgingly. She did not recognize any of the area they were passing through. That was not unusual, she had only been to Springfield once in the past ten years.

The second time she dropped off to sleep the wagon went off the trail and the horses stopped as they faced three big pine trees. She got them back on the road and saw that there were tinges of dawn in the east.

She had another sandwich for breakfast, wishing she could stop to build a fire and make coffee, but she knew she didn't dare. Every mile farther she moved north, was another mile toward safety, and a free and fair life for her children.

The route ran down hill almost all the way so there was no strain on the animals. When sunup came and the chill of the night began to fade, she stopped the rig and roused the children and gave them each a big drink of water from a canvas water bottle and a sandwich to eat.

"Sandwich for breakfast?" Melissa asked.

"Yes," Josh Junior said. "This is a picnic, a

special trip. You be good and don't make trouble."

Mary smiled at her son and got the rig moving again. Soon he was sitting beside her.

"Mom, are they going to come after us, the bad guys who . . . who killed Pa?"

"They might, Josh. Yes. I think they will."

"Then I'm going to be a lookout, a guard. Can I have one of the shotguns?"

"No, Josh, I don't want you being shot. The guns are where I need them." She had put Josh's two six-guns in one of the top boxes. She could get to them if she needed them. She concentrated on driving but got sleepier and sleepier.

"Josh, you drive for a while. When the sun is half way up toward noon, you wake me up."

"Yes, ma'am!" he said and jumped to the seat and took the reins.

She would lay down for just a minute, maybe ten minutes. But it had been a long day and a long night.

Mary slept for two hours before Josh woke her. Mary had a bite of her sandwich and drank some water and felt almost as good as new. Almost.

She had driven down the road a mile more when riders suddenly came out of the brush along both sides of the road. There were three of them. All were laughing and talking. One came close to the right hand side of the wagon.

"Ma'am. This road is closed. I'm afraid you'll have to turn back."

She knew the man, a Bald Knobber.

"Now why would I have to turn back, Wes? Some good reason you can give me?"

"Yes, ma'am. Vern Smith says so. He says he's going to put you in a new house he's setting up. He calls it his five dollar house and there'll be special ladies there for fucking."

She was supposed to be shocked. Mary smiled and reached under the blanket beside her. "Well, in that case, we can't keep Vern waiting, can we. I'm sure he'll be my first customer. I'm charging him twenty dollars." Her hand closed around the shotgun and her finger found the trigger. She pulled it once.

The 12-gauge shotgun shell exploded and a full load of shot blasted through the thin blanket, expanded out of the long barrel into a pattern a foot wide before it caught Wes in the chest.

The force of the shot slammed him off the horse, shattering a dozen ribs, ripping his heart and lungs into a mass of bubbly red froth as he died in mid air even before he hit the ground.

Mary jerked the weapon from under the blanket, swung it a foot to the left and pulled the trigger the second time, dropping the firing pin on the second barrel.

The roar of the gun was louder this time and the target twenty feet farther away, but he took ten pellets into his face, five of them crashing through his nose and eyes directly into his brain, splattering nerve endings, brain tissue and a thousand small blood vessels, jolting the man into eternity while he still slumped forward on the horse.

"Christ!" someone yelled from the other side of the wagon. A pistol fired into the air, and the rider came up fast. He was Hirum Streib, and he was five yards from the wagon but out of the sight lines of the second hidden shotgun.

"What the hell you doing, woman?" he screeched. His six-gun covered her and she let the shotgun drop into her lap. She wanted to throw up, but she knew she couldn't. She had to get Hirum forward more so the second shotgun would kill him.

She had never even hurt another human being before. Now in ten seconds she had killed two men. And she would kill the third one if she had the chance!

Hirum moved his horse forward carefully but stayed out of range of the shotgun.

"Mary, you wouldn't have another scattergun under that blanket, now, would you? Just pick up the blanket easy like. You try to gun me down and you're one dead bitch, I can tell you that. I'm a better shot than your late husband was."

She sat still. If she moved the blanket . . .

"Pull the damn blanket away or I'll shoot your little girl. That get some action?"

"You wouldn't! She's just a child."

"The blanket, Mary. Then you and me gonna have a naked party under the trees over there. Next we'll take the bodies back and let you explain to Vern Smith why we shouldn't hang you for murder."

Mary sighed. It had been a good try. At least it would be two dead for two dead, an eye for an eye. She had avenged her husband's murder. Slowly she took the blanket away from the double barreled Sam Holt breech loader scattergun.

"Yeah, just as I figured. Push it off on the ground. Careful! Right now I'd just about as soon shoot you dead as pull down your panties. Do it!"

She pushed the weapon off the edge of the wagon. It hit the ground and she was surprised it didn't go off.

"Yeah, better. Now stand up and take off that jacket and your shirt. I want to look at me some tits!"

She hesitated.

"Come on, whore, you got nothing to lose now. Might as well use what you got left." He began to laugh as Mary unbuttoned the jacket and took it off.

Behind her a six-gun roared.

She snapped her head around and saw Josh Junior holding one of the big .44's with both hands. She looked at Hirum and he clutched his right shoulder, his gun jolted out of his hand. Almost at once the six-gun fired again, and then a third time, and Mary saw the bullets slam into Hirum Streib's chest, blasting him off the horse and into the soft leaf mold beside the trail.

Josh Junior stood and aimed the weapon at the man lying deathly still on the ground.

"Enough, Josh. Hirum can't hurt us anymore." She stepped off the wagon, picked up the shotgun and put it back in place. Then she looked at the three men. All were dead. She took the guns from their holsters. She could sell them in Springfield.

Back at the wagon, she saw that Josh had picked up the first shotgun and reloaded it. He angled that one to the rear and covered it with part of the blanket he had used last night.

Mary held out her arms and he came to her.

"I know it isn't right to kill anybody, Mama. But . . . but . . ." Then he burst into tears.

She hugged him and let him cry it out. A second later Melissa squirmed against them and Mary held them both. Melissa cried because Josh cried.

She talked softly to them as they sobbed. Told them that sometimes a person has to do something that doesn't look right, but this time it was right. These were bad men who would have taken them back to Branson and done terrible things to them.

"So remember, this was not a bad thing. This was

a good thing. Of course we will never have to do anything like this again, because we will be safe and free of the bad people back in Branson."

She wiped their tears, dug into the food box and came out with apples and gave them each one.

"Now, we have to drive on to Springfield. You kids have never been there. It's really quite a big town. We'll stay there a while and then get on a train and ride all the way to St. Louis."

She kept talking to them for another ten minutes. At last the agony had gone out of Josh's eyes, and he was more relaxed. He wanted to drive again, so she let him.

She figured they had been riding for ten hours. They should be over half way, more than that, thirty miles from Branson. Only another fifteen miles to go. They should be safe now. By the time Vern Smith sent someone to find out what happened to Hirum Streib and his two men, she and the kids would be in Springfield and the wagon unloaded and it and the horses sold.

Mary Newcomb lifted her head and squared her shoulders. She was a lady who could do what had to be done. She wasn't worried any more about what she would find in St. Louis. She would do just fine, thank you, and so would her two children.

# 14

Spur McCoy had been up half the night. He kept a small fire going and boiled a second pot of coffee. By morning most of it was gone. He had watched both women sleeping near the fire on the bough beds. They were exhausted.

Edith was content to stay at or in the cave until Spur was ready to ride for Springfield. He and Priscilla had argued for an hour after Edith went to sleep. There was no way he could convince her not to go back into Branson.

After she went to sleep, he nursed his java by the fire and tried to come up with some plan of attack that would put a crimp in the Bald Knobbers' power, yet still let him keep his oath as a peace officer.

It was nearly morning when he had the spark of an idea and he drifted off to sleep leaning against his saddle to let the idea germinate and grow while he slept.

Priscilla was up before he was and had a fresh pot of coffee boiling and bacon and hash browns cooking.

"Sorry we're out of eggs," she said as he wiped the sleep from his eyes.

"Put it on my tab and buy a couple of dozen," he said. He went out to the spring to wash up, and came back hungry and with the new idea worked out well enough to get it moving.

As he entered the cave, he saw Priscilla getting ready to ride out.

"Don't go," Spur said. "You've made your point. You've paid them back two for one. It's too risky to try for Vern Smith. He may even be the head Bald Knobber by now."

"It really doesn't matter," Priscilla said slowly. "We had no children to worry about. I can take the risk. I won the first two times, there's no reason why I shouldn't come away unscratched this time as well."

"There are several good reasons," Spur said. "It's going to be broad daylight. You might not be able to catch Vern Smith alone. By now he almost certainly is armed everywhere he goes. He may even have a Bald Knobber or two as bodyguards."

"He might just have a chance then. But I have all day. I can wait until I find the right moment."

"Wait ten minutes and I'll ride part way into town with you."

Priscilla grinned and her dimples popped in, her eyes danced. "You thought of a way to blast the Knobbers and still stay a lawman?"

"Working on it. What do you know about the preacher?"

Priscilla laughed. "Yes, good idea! He isn't the best preacher in the world. Non-denominational. His name is Dutch Van Aken. As far as I heard he never took sides on the Knobbers. No praise, no damning them. Sounds like a good man to start with for some kind of local resistance to the Knobbers."

Spur and the two women ate the breakfast of bread and jam, hashbrowns and bacon, then Edith waved them off.

"I'll do the cleanup and get everything ready to ride. You two be back before dawn so we can get a head start in the dark." She laughed. "I have an easier time hiding in the dark than you two will."

Spur and Priscilla led their mounts out through the hidden entrance, made sure the brush and branches swung back in position, and then mounted and rode.

They talked little until they could see the town. Then Spur stopped and rubbed his stubbled chin. He was still in his disguise as a down and outer.

"One last shot, Priscilla. Don't go in there. You're too pretty a woman to be risked in this kind of a game. I should tie you up right here and pick you up on my way back."

"You wouldn't dare!" she snapped. Then she grinned. "McCoy, relax. You've got two women, one of us is bound to be around for you to make passionate love to after this is over."

"Don't joke about it, Priscilla. I know you're still furious about their hanging your husband, but now is the time to use your head, too."

"Not a chance, McCoy. I've got one more man to kill. See you back at the cave." She waved, kicked her mount in the flanks and rode away from him angling more to the south so she could come in through the least populated section of town.

Spur sat there for fifteen minutes watching her until she was out of sight. Then he nudged his horse into motion and rode through all the cover he could find to the west side of town, and left his horse in some brush. He carried only the new six-gun he had taken from the hardware store.

His clothes were mud caked and dirty. He had discarded the blue shirt, and wore a brown one that was as filthy as his pants. The same slouch hat perched on his head and another day's black stubble growth made him look like anybody but Spur McCoy.

He waded in the creek for a dozen yards to soak his boots and pants legs to the knees. He came out of the brush beside the creek and slanted to the start of a street. No one seemed to notice him. He shuffled down to the first alley, and walked into it, peering into a trash barrel as if looking for some discarded food.

A merchant chased him away from his trash box. On down the alley he saw the church steeple, and he turned on the next street and went around to the church's back door. The parsonage was next to the white building, and he knocked on the rear door there.

A slender man with spectacles on answered his call. The man wore a high collar and garters around his dress shirt sleeves. He had a thin moustache, and suspenders on blue serge pants.

"My good fellow, our poor box is empty this week. I might find you a bit of breakfast, but that would be about all."

"Reverend Van Aken, I'm not here to beg or for breakfast. I need to talk to you about an urgent matter. May I come in?"

"Yes, yes, of course. I didn't mean to insult you. Your appearance . . . "

"Understood. Can we talk inside?"

The parson hesitated only a second. "Yes, of course." He pushed open the door. "Come in, we can talk privately here in the kitchen. I'm a widower."

"Sorry. Rev. Van Aken. There is a serious

problem in this town that I'm sure you're aware of, the Bald Knobbers. You must know how they have taken over the entire county, run it the way they feel, kill anyone they don't like." Spur stopped. "Sorry, you know the whole story better than I do. I want you to help me do something about it."

The preacher frowned. "Just what could we do? I don't understand."

"We need an opposing force. We need to rally the honest and God-fearing men of town so they will face up to the thieves and killers who run the county. If we could get fifty men to line up on one side of the street with their pistols and rifles, and show that they were willing to go to war to save their county, I'm sure the Bald Knobbers would pull up their stakes and walk off their claim."

The preacher took off his glasses, removed a handkerchief from his pocket and polished the ground glass.

"Well, I guess it's possible. But most of our churchgoers are not the kind of men who would be good fighters."

"We won't have to fight, that's the glory of the plan," Spur said. "We get the men to meet and form a power group and then we put on a show of strength and the Knobbers will have to back down."

"Interesting, yes, interesting. I'm sorry I didn't catch your name."

"True, I didn't give it."

"Why are you so concerned about our town? I don't remember seeing you around here before."

"I've only been here for two days, Reverend Van Aken. But in those two days, two innocent men have been killed by the Bald Knobbers, and I understand two of the Knobbers have been killed by some irate citizen."

"I see. That still doesn't explain your interest in our town. We're a small place. You just riding through?"

Spur took a deep breath. If this were going to work, he had to take some chances. "Rev. Van Aken, I came into town trailing Sam Bass and his bank robbing gang, then I lost them. The sheriff wouldn't cooperate with me when I caught two of them, and then all sorts of wild things began to happen.

"Mr. Van Aken, I'm a United States Secret Service Agent, sworn to uphold all the laws of this land. That's why I'm so interested in seeing some justice returned to Branson."

"Well, I am surprised and delighted. You must be in disguise then. Do you have a name?"

"Yes. I'm Spur McCoy, which I afraid is an unpopular name now in Branson with the authorities."

"Well, well, well! Yes, I have heard that name bandied about. Now, let's see what we can do about gathering a list of men.. The church membership rolls would be the place to start."

"Sounds helpful."

"Mr. McCoy, I'll need to get them from the other room. Why don't we move into my study. It's a bit messy I'm afraid. Oh, no, the records are in the church office. I'll only be a minute. Sit down here in my chair and I'll be right back."

Spur sat on a chair in the cluttered study that had a big desk littered with papers, a wall filled with books, and a wall hanging that had been hand worked in cross stitch showing the Twenty Third Psalm. Spur stood and walked around the room.

He passed the window and saw the preacher walking toward the house on the far side of the church. He returned to the church and a minute later came in the back door and then the study with a large black book.

"Here it is, church history and membership book. Dates back to well before the war, near as I can tell about seventeen eighty-five." He moved to the pages half way through.

"Now here is the current membership."

As he spoke two men came into the room's open door. One had out a six-gun and he aimed it at Spur.

"Not a twitch, McCoy, or you'll be dead meat in a pine box."

Spur sprang forward, grabbed the preacher who did not move fast enough to clear the gunman's target. Spur used the minister as a shield, then kicked forward and the gun flew out of the man's hand.

Spur drew his own .44 and the weapon responded to his figner pressure and the second man in the doorway with a gun out toppled into the hallway halfway to heaven before the sound of the weapon faded.

"On the floor, now!" Spur thundered at the first gunman still holding his half-broken wrist. The man went down. "Hands over your head, lace your fingers!"

Spur spun the preacher around. The benign look that had been there before was now replaced with a snarl.

"Damn! I should have gut shot you when I had the chance," the preacher said.

"Van, I done just what you said, I tried hard," the man on the floor whined.

"Shut up, fool!"

Spur slammed his pistol down across the preacher's face. The man groaned. Spur felt up and down his body, found no weapon and pushed him to the floor. He picked up the dropped pistols from both men, then aimed at the minister's face with his hogsleg.

"Who are the top three leaders of the Knobbers, Van Aken? Tell me now and live another five minutes."

"No. I can't. They'd kill me."

Spur kicked him in the side just over his kidney. The preacher doubled up in pain. Spur waited.

"Another minute, Van Aken, then you'll find out for sure if there is life after death."

"No! no. I'll tell you." He gasped for breath and shuddered, then swallowed. "Abe Conners was top man. Then Vern Smith the Banker moved up. I guess Hirum Streib is next in line and then I'm the next."

"You've been a Knobber all the time?"

"Since I came to town, five years ago."

"And you're not a real preacher?"

"Hell, no! Abe and me rode in. We heard about the new preacher coming, so we met him at the stage outside of town, took him off and damned if his clothes didn't fit me tolerable good. That preacher didn't need them six feet under where he was by then. I keep track of the brethren this way."

"You used to keep track of them," Spur said. He looked at the first man on the floor, then back at the preacher. All he saw was a blur of the fake religious man's right hand as it swung up a derringer and fired. Spur's reflexes triggered a shot at the phony minister that caught him in the forehead and killed him instantly.

The derringer's round slashed past Spur's cheek and punctured the wall hanging. Spur aimed at the other man, then he let the hammer down easy.

"Bald Knobber, you're through in this town. You get to a horse and get on it, and ride like hell out of town. I see you around here in an hour and I'm putting five slugs through your left eye. You understand me, scum bag?"

"Yes . . . yes. Yes sir. I can . . . I can be gone in half an hour . . . easy."

"Don't tell anybody what happened here. You savvy?"

The man nodded. He shivered so hard he could barely stand. Spur kicked him in the butt as he ran out the door. Spur faded through the back door and down the alley. Nobody had wondered why there had been three shots in the preacher's house.

Spur took his time, looked in garbage cans, trash barrels, got run off by another merchant, and at last wandered to Main Street and turned down toward the bank.

There was only one left in town, the Branson First Bank. It sat on the corner, looked substantial with its solid brick construction, and two big windows so people could see there was no funny business going on inside with their money.

Spur hunkered down on his heels and leaned against the front of the hardware store.

Within ten minutes he had heard about the store owner's hanging, and how his wife had raced out of town last night just after dark. The note was still tacked to the door. Spur read it, then squatted down again and leaned against the wall.

Evidently the Bald Knobbers were so nervous they hung one of their own men. Doc Gibson was acting for the widow. Maybe he was an honest man. Maybe.

Spur had been watching the bank, but nowhere did he see a redheaded woman who looked like a young boy, who had a grudge to kill the banker. Spur waited another half hour, then he rose, stretched, got outraged looks from two matrons and ambled off down the alley to find the doctor's office.

The place was a block down on Main. Half of the building was where the doctor lived, the other half his office space. There was no nurse, no receptionist, just a bell over the door and a pad of paper for the patient to write down his name and his complaint.

Spur wrote down George Washington, for the name, and sudden death syndrome—hanging, as the complaint. There was no one else in the waiting room.

Spur put the pad of paper back on the small stand and waited. A minute later a man came in dressed in tan pants and a white shirt with the sleeves rolled up. He wore glasses and looked first at the pad.

He saw the name and glanced up, saw Spur and grinned, then looked at the complaint. The doctor frowned, motioned Spur with him and tore off the sheet of paper and wadded it up. They went to a small room and the doctor closed the door.

"Doctor Gibson?" Spur asked.

"Yes, George, bad problem you have."

"Isn't mine, Doctor, it's the town's problem. I want to do something about it, any suggestions?"

The man in front of him rubbed his hand across his face. "You're here because of the note on the hardware store door. That figures. The Knobbers might figure it too, but somebody had to help that lady. I just hope to God she makes it."

"You helped her get out of town?"

"Yes. This morning I heard Vern Smith sent out three men to bring her back."

The doctor stared at Spur again. "Saw you one

day. Your real name must be McCoy, Spur McCoy. That's got to mean you're some kind of federal lawman. Don't matter. Not anything legal you can do here."

The man lifted his head and stared at Spur. "Unless you're the one who cut down Barney Figuroa and Abe Conners."

"That pleasure was not mine."

"Then who?"

"You might not believe me, Doc."

The doctor walked around the room. "The only other person would be the Negro girl, Edith, I think her name was. Or . . . Mrs. Russell, Priscilla Russell."

Spur shrugged. "Doctor, what else can the town do? I figured the preacher would be a good man to approach. Turns out he's the third man in line to run the Bald Knobbers."

"Van Aken? Well, mercy me."

"He isn't even a real preacher. He told me he and Abe Conners waylaid and killed the real preacher and Van Aken took over his Bible, his clothes and his church."

"What won't they do next?"

"Without their leadership would they wither up and die out?"

"Possible."

"I've got a hunch Vern Smith might not live out the day. That leaves Hirum Streib."

"Streib in line too?"

"Third or fourth."

"He's a no account."

"Fight them, Doc. Set up a Committee For Justice, get honest men and run the hooligans out of town. You got a lot fewer now to worry about."

"What about the sheriff?"

"He should be run out too. Trouble is he was duly elected."

"Election was fixed, don't mean a spoon full of beans," Doc said. He paced the office again. "If we could do it without more of the innocents getting killed, I'd try." He stared at Spur a minute.

"McCoy, Sheriff Parcheck arrested you, violated your rights, misused his office. You can arrest him on a federal charge and haul him off to Springfield. You get him out of town and we'll figure out how to take care of Streib and the rest of the Knobbers. We can even deal with Vern Smith."

Just then somebody came in the front door and rang the bell.

"Doc! Doc! Come quick. Some crazy woman just shot down Vern Smith. He looks deader than hell!"

"That would be Priscilla Russell," Spur said. The doctor took off running. Spur ambled up the street in the same direction.

# 15

Priscilla Russell adjusted her shirt again so her bound breasts would not show and swung down off her horse at the edge of town. No use attracting any more attention than needed. She did not wear a gunbelt, it would look out of place on her. Instead she carried a small box that held the .44 Colt pistol.

This time she was a young boy going on an errand. No one would glance twice at her. She had smeared mud on one cheek to detract from her clear-skinned look, and she had not washed on purpose this morning.

She still made a girlish looking boy of about sixteen, but it would have to do.

Priscilla had thought a lot about what Spur had told her. That Vern Smith especially would be watching for someone to try to kill him. He knew he was the third one on the lynching party that had hung Phillip Russell, and Vern was the only one left alive. He would try to keep it that way.

She walked along the street toward Main, dragging a stick in the dust the way she had seen countless boys do. She watched the people but not obviously.

Phillip Russell's widow knew Vern Smith by sight, that was one big advantage. He didn't know who was trying to kill him. Surely he would not suspect her. She sat down on the boardwalk with her feet in the street a foot below, and watched the town. She had never really stopped and studied it.

People were rushing every which way, just like they had something important to do.

Main Street. Horses, wagons, buggies, a few people meandering along on the boardwalks. Each merchant built his own walk in front of his store. Some met flush, some were higher or lower than the one next to it. Most of the boardwalks were eight to twelve inches above the dust and dirt, and often mud, of the raw dirt street.

Down a block she could see the Branson First Bank solidly stationed on the corner. Nobody came or went from it yet. It would not open until ten. Why did bankers keep such short hours, she wondered.

A sudden chill slanted through her. For a moment she remembered the agony, the horrendous fear in Abe Conners' eyes when he knew he was going to die. Now Abe was dead, but so was Phillip! Somebody else was going to die today, and Priscilla prayed that it would be Vern Smith.

She frowned. That was no such thing to be praying for. For a moment she felt remors, then she closed her mind to it. No! Vern Smith had killed wantonly, he deserved to die. And she was the only person who could exact that deadly vengeance. It would be done!

She stood and wandered up the street. For a while she sat outside the saloon trying to listen to what the men were saying.

"Hanging," she heard the word again. Then she looked the other way down the street toward the hotel and saw it. A man had been hanged to the big black oak near the hotel. His body slowly turned in the morning breeze.

The name came then, Josh Newcomb, the hardware man. They had struck again. But she thought that Josh had been with the Bald Knobbers, not against them.

Soon she found out about Mrs. Newcomb taking a wagon and running away in the night with her two children. Silently Priscilla grieved with the new widow, then prayed that she would get safely to Springfield.

Two men went into the bank. She wondered what time it was. A clock in the next store, a big Seth Thomas striking clock that was for sale, showed that it was ten twelve. The bank was open! She was sure that by now Vern had to be inside.

Back door. He would come in a rear entrance. She stared at the bank. How should she do it? Should she wander in looking around, curious. Find Smith, open the box and shoot him? By now she was sure everyone in the bank would be armed. Even the tellers.

She walked past the bank slowly. Tried to hit a tossed up stone with the stick but missed. She stared inside. All boys are curious. She saw one customer, and the usual partition and the tellers' cages. No Vern Smith. He would be behind a desk.

She had been in the bank only once before to sign some papers with her husband. Slowly, she walked on past. Down the side street she could find no back door to the bank. Not even on the alley. One way in, one way out.

For a flash of a second she wondered that maybe

Spur McCoy was right. Maybe two for one was enough.

"No!" she said sharply out loud. She looked around, but there was no one near her. She retraced her steps to Main and went to the far side of the street and sat in the shade. More people came and went from the bank.

Priscilla sat up straight, her whole body quivering. A man had just left the bank. It was Vern Smith. He wore a six-gun on his hip. A man followed him closely with two guns looking at everyone in front and behind Smith. A bodyguard.

She gripped the box tightly. Smith walked the other way, down three doors and vanished into the saloon called the Bar--B. She frowned. She could not walk into the bar. The apron would toss her out as being too young. She had to wait for Vern to get up his Dutch courage and come back out.

Suddenly she was hungry. A good cup of coffee would be fine right now. Money? Did she bring any money with her? She had taken all the cash from her house when she fled with Spur—about twelve dollars. But she had brought none in her pants pockets with her.

For a minute she had an urge to walk up the block and look at the house she and Phil had bought the first week they were in town. What a mistake that had been! She knew there was no time for her to look at the house. She could miss Vern. She slouched on the boardwalk, then went to a string of empty chairs backed up against the Branson General store and sat in one of them.

It was only fifteen minutes later that Vern Smith came out of the saloon, hurried to the bank and went inside. The bodyguard walked two steps behind him all the way.

Priscilla knew she should have a plan. She knew that she should be near the bank and wait for him to come out. But planning was not her best talent. She stood, brushed off her pants, saw that her shirt did not have breasts bumps in it and walked toward the bank.

A cold sweat touched her forehead but she ignored it. Now was the time. She had no reason to put it off. She might get hurt in there, but there was no other way. She would walk in, find Vern and shoot him. Then she would worry about trying to get out.

Not that it mattered that much.

The important job was to kill Vern Smith!

Each step seemed like a mile now as she walked the half block down the street. For a minute she waited for two wagons to pass, then stepped off the boardwalk into the dust of the street and went around horse droppings to the far side.

The bank was two doors down.

Priscilla took a deep breath, checked the box. Yes, the top flipped off and the weapon was there. She had cocked it so all she had to do was aim and pull the trigger—no squeeze it. She would be so close she couldn't miss.

The door was heavy.

A man reached beside her and pushed the door open, then they both were in the bank. It had a fancy tile floor and varnished teller cages with real metal bars in front of them.

She looked around.

Two tellers stared at her, dismissed her and she walked to the far end, away from the tellers. There was a door there and a desk in front of it. No one sat at the desk. She didn't see the bodyguard with the two guns.

Priscilla paused a minute at the desk, then walked

to the door. It had to be Vern Smith's office. Then she saw the plaque on the door that said: President, Vern Smith.

She moved quickly, grabbed the knob and turned, thrusting it open. Inside she saw Vern look up from his desk. The man with two guns was behind him. They both frowned at her for interrupting them.

"Yes, son?" Vern said. "Do you want to open an account or maybe take out a loan?"

Vern laughed and the bodyguard laughed. She turned with her back to them, opened the box and grabbed the weapon. When she spun around she swung up the gun and fired. The first round killed the bodyguard.

She thumbed the hammer back and before Smith could reach for his gun, she fired again. The bullet went through his heart and he fell dead on his desk.

Priscilla let out a held in breath, dropped the six-gun on the floor and turned for the door.

The teller nearest the president's office had heard the first shot and he grabbed a sawed-off shotgun and raced to the door. He saw the boy fire the second shot and turn. The teller stared at the boy for just a second, then pulled both triggers.

The twin shotgun blasts from only six feet away tore into Priscilla's man's shirt and blasted away half of her abdomen, almost cutting her in half. Her body flew backward against the desk, and then slid to the floor. Blood and bits of flesh and clothing sprayed over the back wall and the desk.

The teller ran to Smith and saw that he was dead. He checked the guard. There was no reason to look at the boy. By the time he turned the door the other two bank workers were there.

"Close the bank," he said calmly. "Send someone for Doc Gibson and the sheriff." Then the teller slumped to the floor and threw up.

The sheriff got there before Doc Gibson did. He had closed the bank and kept everyone out. Doc Gibson checked the three and shook his head.

"All dead, Lund, you should have known that. Nothing I can do for any of them." Doc stared at the bloodied remains of the boy. He reached down and pulled off the old hat. A riot of shoulder length red hair tumbled out. Doc wiped the smudge off the cheek.

"Here's your vicious killer, Sheriff. Her name is Priscilla Russell, the widow of the man Vern Smith and two others hanged a few days ago. Guess it's an eye for an eye, wouldn't you say?"

Sheriff Parcheck stared at the woman.

"Christ! I don't believe it! She had the guts to walk in here and blast Doug and then Vern, in broad daylight?"

"Looks so, Sheriff. I'd wager she's the one who shot both Abe and Barney too. From what I hear those three are the ones who hanged her husband."

Doc stood there a minute. "What you going to do now, Sheriff?"

"Well, guess we should get these bodies over to the undertaker. Or have him come get them. Yeah, his job." The sheriff walked out of the bank like a ship that had lost its sail. He had no one left in the Knobber group to tell him what to do. Doc Gibson snorted and wondered if Spur McCoy had some surprises fixed up for the sheriff. He hoped so.

Spur McCoy munched on a square of four big cinnamon rolls he had bought at the bakery and lounged against the side of the bank. He had heard what happened inside. The bank teller had revived and was telling everyone.

Then the word rocketed through the street that

the killer had been a woman, not a boy. It was Priscilla Russell, the young lawyer's widow.

Spur relaxed in the sun. When Doc Gibson came out, he fell into step beside him.

"Priscilla?" he asked.

"Yep. Blown half in two with a shotgun. Damn messy. Nothing I could do."

"Damn it to hell!" Spur shouted at no one, at every one. "I told her not to try it, but the only way I could have stopped her was to tie her up. I don't tie up pretty ladies." Spur walked for several paces in silence. "The sheriff seems a bit unsure of himself."

Doc Gibson was grim. "He damn well should be. The top three leaders of the Knobbers are dead. He's worried he might be next. And now he doesn't have anyone to tell him exactly what to do every minute. He might not be able to get his pants on tomorrow without someone to tell him how."

"I'll tell him how. By then I'll have arrested him for a variety of charges and have him on his way to Springfield and points east."

Doc stopped. "You truth telling?"

"Damn right. Then the Knobbers will have no leaders, they will not even have the appearance of legality, and you should be able to put together an interim county government that can last until you call a special, honest election."

"Sounds good. Damn't, I know four or five who will help me. We'll tack up a notice that any former members of the Bald Knobbers have twenty-four hours to get out of town or face arrest. Then we appoint a temporary sheriff and get a bunch of county councilmen or supervisors or whatever they're called. Lots of work to do."

"Serves you right for volunteering," Spur said.

Spur dug into his dirty pants and came up with a

gold double eagle. "Would you see to the funeral for Priscilla? She deserves a marker and all."

Doc nodded. "Glad to. That little lady had more nerve and will power than most of the men I know. She had to figure if she got to Vern that she'd never come out of the bank alive. Still she marched in there and took out a fast gun bodyguard and Vern before he could get off a shot."

Spur shook hands with the doctor, turned down a side street where he found a horse trough. He washed off his hands and face, wiped dry with his hands and adjusted the gun on his belt.

Now he had to have a run-in with the sheriff. He hoped the man was still there and had not cleared out of town.

Before Spur got to the sheriff's office a man rode into town leading three horses. Over each horse a dead man had been tied. Men ran to the street and lifted heads to identify the men.

"Wally Perkins," one man said. "Shotgun blasted him into kingdom come."

"Turk Johnson," another voice said. "Another shotgun I'd say."

"Shit, look at this! Old Hirum Streib done caught himself two slugs. One dead through the heart."

"Where you want them?" the stranger said. "I come on them back down the trail, and rushed right along to get here. Nobody else around. Did see some fresh wagon tracks though, heading toward Springfield."

Sheriff Parcheck ran up and looked at the bodies. When he saw Streib's body his shoulders sagged.

"Take them over to the undertaker. He's gonna have more business than he knows what to do with."

Spur knew Hirum Streib was a Bald Knobber, one

of the leaders. These could have been the three men Vern Smith sent to bring back the widow Newcomb and her kids. If so that meant there were three more Knobbers down and dead. That could be eleven of them in graves already. The rest of the hard core must be having serious doubts by now about the whole movement.

Spur caught up with the sheriff just as he went inside his office. Spur looked around and saw no one else in the small room.

"Sheriff Parcheck. I understand that you're looking for me." Spur pulled his gun and covered the lawman. "My name is Spur McCoy and you're under arrest for violation of laws of the United States, and of this state and county."

# 16

Sheriff Lund Parcheck stared at Spur in disbelief. "You . . . yeah, maybe you are. Clean you up a lot. What the hell's the weapon for?"

"Parcheck, you're under arrest for kidnapping, assault and battery, malfeasance in office, giving a bribe, taking a bribe, violation of citizens rights, grand larceny and for being an absolute asshole."

"You're joking. I'm the law in Taney county."

"You were, right back this way to the jail cells. Remember what happened to the four top leaders in the Bald Knobbers, Parcheck. They are all dead, along with seven more of the Knobbers. You want to make it twelve instead of eleven?"

"Knobbers? I ain't one of them. I'm the duly elected sheriff of Taney county."

"Election was rigged, only one man allowed to file and run. Move it, Parcheck. I want you locked up safe and sound." Spur grabbed a ring of keys off the desk and pushed the man to the hallway and down the row of cells. He shoved Parcheck in the second cell, slammed the door and locked it, made sure there was nobody else in the jail and went back to the front office.

Two men stood there. "Who the hell're you?" one asked.

"New deputy," Spur said.

"Better take a bath and get some clean clothes."

"Just as soon as I get my first pay day."

"Where's the sheriff?"

"Busy at the minute. Said I should talk to anybody."

"We ain't just anybody." One of them shut the front door.

"Yeah, we special friends. We need to know what the hell to do now. Everybody been killed off. Who's in charge? Who sits at the table?"

"Got the answer right back here, boys," Spur said, drawing his iron. "Just ease them shooters out and put them on the floor, nice and slow like." One of the men started to draw, and Spur slammed a bullet into the floor an inch from his boot.

"Easy, next one goes in your balls. Put down the iron!"

Both did. "What the hell is this?" one of them asked.

"Change of command, boys. The Knobbers are all through in Taney county. Some of the good old boys took off, most are dead. You can stay if you want to volunteer to dig your own grave."

"Told you we shoulda rode for Springfield," the shorter one growled.

Spur prodded them into the first cell, locked it and let them yell at the sheriff. Back out front, Spur locked the outside door and went to Doc Gibson's office. He was setting a boy's leg. Spur helped hold the leg straight as Doc wrapped on the bandages, then lathered them with a half inch of plaster of paris cast.

When the cast was done, they sat in a small office.

"Doc, we got something of a problem. No sheriff. I just arrested him. I'm appointing you as chairman of the Temporary Governing Committee. You have until five o'clock to get five members, and then until six to appoint a new interim sheriff. Your mandate is to have elections within three months to fill all of the vacancies in the county government."

"Spur, I'm not a politician."

"Good, that's why this is a temporary appointment. In three months your job is over and the county will have a government."

Doc rubbed his chin. "I did say I'd take a stab at it if you got rid of Sheriff Parcheck." He walked around the office once, then thrust out his hand. "Deal, McCoy. How soon do you need a new sheriff?"

"About twenty minutes ago."

Doc hesitated. "What's going to happen to Parcheck?"

"I figured like you that he couldn't get an honest trial in Missouri, so I'm taking him down into Arkansas to stand trial. Him and two more Knobbers. At least we're going to start that way. I've got an idea how we might smoke out some more of the hooded characters."

"You hold down the jail for half an hour and I'll have a new sheriff for you. He's a good man. Used to be a lawman back east, then came out here. Honest as the long cold of winter. Name is Cully Jacobson, about thirty. Now git."

Spur grinned as he left the doctor's office. It was getting along to afternoon. He bought a fresh apple pie at the same bakery as before and ate it all on his way to the jail. Inside the three prisoners were yelling.

Spur pushed open the door. "Any more screeching back here and nobody gets any supper. Understood?"

When he closed the door all was quiet.

Cully Jacobson came in a short time later. He was a strongly built man, with a moustache and close cut hair. He wore a .44 with a long leather holster that hid a long barrel. Cully grinned.

"Hear I'm the new, temporary sheriff," he said.

"Soon as I swear you in. This is for not more than three months, and you do right by these people, or I'll come back here and kick your ass all over the county."

"Sounds right by me," Cully said. "I done some law work back in Kansas, about five years ago."

Spur swore him in, not sure if he had the power, but knowing it would be a million times better than what Taney county used to have.

"My only orders are that you do no executions. Nobody is hanged in the county until a proper group of elected officials take over."

"Fine."

"Right now you have three prisoners. One is the former sheriff, and right hand man of the Bald Knobbers. The other two are Knobbers. I'm taking all three down to Arkansas tomorrow so they can have a fair and just trial."

"Feed them twice a day and charge it to the county at whichever cafe or eatery will hold the tab."

Spur sat down at the desk and motioned the new sheriff in closer. "Now this is what I have planned for tomorrow. I'll need your help and that of two friends you can trust with your life."

Ten minutes later, Spur walked out on Branson's Main Street and it seemed to feel different. There were more people moving around. He saw that the Newcomb hardware store was open and busy. The stage pulled in and two people got off and three got on. Two of them were men eager to leave town.

Spur walked out to his horse and rode back to the cave, getting there slightly before dark. He told Edith what had happened to Priscilla. Edith cried.

"I was getting to like that lady. She was so strong and proud. I don't think I could ever use a gun the way she did."

Edith had cooked some beans, after soaking them all morning, and mixed in the rest of the bacon before it spoiled. They had a good meal, and Spur told her she could come back to town if she wanted to. She shook her head.

"No, too many bad, bad memories. I'm ready to ride to Springfield and get back home, though. When can we go?"

"Day after tomorrow," Spur said. "If all goes well tomorrow in town, and outside of town."

"Are you really going to take the former sheriff and those two Knobbers all the way to Arkansas for a trail?"

"Might, but I don't think we'll get that far."

"Oh."

They cleaned up the supper things, Spur watered both horses and tied them outside where they could eat some grass. Then they talked for a while sitting around an easy fire.

"I've never known a white man like you before," she said. "Now, I've not known a lot of white men, but most of them were overly polite, or downright rude. You treat me just like any other person."

"Hey! didn't mean to. You are a special lady. The way you stood up to those goons was wonderful. You're strong and you believe in standing up for your rights. You just tried once in the wrong place."

They went to bed early. Spur had settled down when she brought over her blankets and lay beside him. She put her hand on his shoulder.

"Spur McCoy. I'm not trying to seduce you, I . . . I just want to touch you, know you're there. Do you mind?"

Spur laughed softly. "No, just be careful where you touch. Lying here so close to a beautiful, sexy lady could get me all worked up."

"I'll be careful. But maybe tomorrow night I won't be so careful."

Spur leaned over and kissed her lips softly, then turned away.

"Pretty lady, that is a definite appointment."

The next morning, Spur rode to town early, had a big breakfast at a small cafe and got to the sheriff's office at 7:30. The new sheriff was there, having slept overnight on a cot in the hallway.

"McCoy, I got one man to go with you. We'll have the prisoners handcuffed so they can ride and the horses tied together. Shouldn't be much of a problem getting over the old Indian trail through the Ozarks and down to a place called Harrison. About thirty-five miles or so and county seat of Boone County."

Spur walked around the three horses and the one man who was to ride with him. Both he and the other man had a sack of provisions on the back of their horses. It was a two day ride so they wouldn't take much food. The three prisoners sat glumly on the horses, their wrists bound together with shackles.

"Special deputy Roger Zilke is your guard," the new sheriff said. "He's a good man with a rifle."

"Looks like we're ready," Spur said. He changed horses, mounted up on the loaded bay and led the contingent out across the street and south out Main toward the old Indian trail. There was little traffic between the two states at this point since there were only small towns on each side.

Spur talked briefly with Zilke, then the guard moved to the back of the line of three prisoners.

"Long damn way from here to Boone County, McCoy," Parcheck said.

"Yeah. Maybe we should make you walk. You want to walk, Parcheck?"

The former sheriff made no reply, just glared at Spur and they kept riding. As they rode out of sight, Doc Gibson stood beside the new sheriff.

"Damn, I hope it goes the way we want it to go," Cully said.

Doc Gibson scratched his ear. "Way he set it up, should work. All we can do now is wait and see."

Spur led the men along the trail for half an hour. Branson was well behind them. He came to a gully where they had to start a climb toward a low pass ahead, where Spur called a halt.

"Dang horse threw a shoe or something," Spur said, getting down. He lifted the mount's foot and led her to the side and tied her reins to a bush.

"You men get down," Spur ordered. "We'll tie you to a tree. I think this broken down nag needs a slight rest, then we should be able to move again. Zilke, start a small fire and let's have some coffee. No sense wasting a half hour."

The coffee was brewed and Spur stretched out next to a fallen pine tree. Zilke had taken a cup of coffee, laid his repeating rifle over his knees and squatted beside a two foot thick shortleaf pine.

Spur kept working lower and lower until he was perfectly protected from two sides by the big log.

It came a little later than Spur figured it would. Three rifle shots blasted into their small camp. One nicked the log behind where Spur lay, and the second one caught the tip of Zilke's boot but did no damage.

Parcheck and the two prisoners dropped into the dirt as low as they could go.

There was a whoop from above them on the sides of the ravine. Six more shots slammed into the rocks around the five men huddled behind whatever cover they could find.

Parcheck screamed in delight. "Come get them, boys! Only two of them here. One's behind the log. Circle around and nail his ass. Zilke is over by the big tree."

Spur pushed his hat up over the log on the barrel of his Winchester repeater. A rifle round slammed through his low-crowned topper, spinning it around. He pulled it down.

"Damn, that was a new hat!"

A dozen more shots came into the area.

"You all right, Zilke?" Spur called.

"Fine, no problem. Where is the damn cavalry?"

As he said it they heard shots from higher on the slope from both sides.

"What the hell is that?" Parcheck yelled.

"The cavalry, Parcheck. Greetings for your friends up on the side of the hill. How many you have up there, three or four? I hear the rest of the Knobbers rode out of town last night."

The rounds stopped coming at the men below. The battle raged above now, as the Knobbers fought with someone higher on the hills. A scream echoed down the canyon.

A dozen more shots, then the sound of one horse charging away. Before any of them below could move, six more shots jolted into the rocks, with the hot lead bouncing off the boulders every which way.

A scream from one of the prisoners, and then all was quiet.

"McCoy!" a voice called from above.

"All right down here," he yelled back.

"We nailed two of the bastards, one took off, but he's heading south. Good chance we'll never see him again."

"Good work. Take the bodies back into town. We'll be along directly."

Spur stood and looked around. Two of the prisoners were flat on the ground rolled into small balls. Parcheck lay sprawled behind a small boulder that wasn't big enough to protect him.

"Parcheck, you all right?" Spur called. The Secret Agent walked over and nudged the ex-sheriff. When Spur rolled him over he saw where two slugs had cut into Parcheck's chest. He was dead.

One of the prisoners caught a ricochetting round and had a small gash on his upper leg.

Spur took the handcuffs off both men.

"Now take off your shirt and tie up that leg wound," Spur told the man.

"Just get me back to town, Doc Gibson can fix it," the man snarled.

"You aren't going back to town," Spur told the man. He ordered both of them to strip naked, boots, everything. Zilke picked up the clothes, tied them in a bundle and tied the boots together, then lashed them to the saddle of one of the horses.

When the man's thigh wound was wrapped, Spur pointed to the south.

"That way, Bald Knobbers. It's less than forty miles to the first town. When you get there you can worry about what to do about clothes." He tossed them a four inch knife with a folding blade.

"You should be able to live off the land for a few days. Have a nice walk."

"You can't do this!" the unwounded man roared.

"Can't?" Spur said moving toward him. "Maybe you'd like one of your heel tendons cut so you can't walk right. You want that?" The man moved away shaking his head.

Spur motioned with his pistol and made the men walk past Parcheck.

"Consider yourselves lucky. You could have caught a slug like Parcheck did. You suppose those Bald Knobbers up there shot him on purpose?"

Spur yelled at the two prisoners and they hurried up the trail, picking their way carefully on tender feet.

Together Spur and Zilke loaded the ex-sheriff on his horse, belly down, and tied his hands and feet together under the nag's belly. Then they mounted up and sent two rifle shots at the naked Knobbers who worked up the canyon toward the pass at the top. They would be able to see into Arkansas from there.

"That pair will never set foot in Missouri again, I'd wager a year's pay," Zilke said.

"Let's hope so," Spur said and led the string of horses with one dead man back toward town.

The three dead Bald Knobbers were laid out in a row outside the sheriff's office. Kin was invited to claim the bodies. Nobody did. The new sheriff called some of the onlookers together and told them about the attack in the mountains.

"Parcheck got killed, the other two prisoners escaped, and two of the attacking force were killed. That accounts for at least fourteen of the hard core of the Bald Knobbers who controlled this county for so long. From now on, justice and law is going to prevail in this county. Anybody has any problems with that way of life, this is an invite to mount up and ride out."

The sheriff turned his back on the crowd and walked into the office to clapping and shouts of approval.

Spur McCoy bought Doc Gibson a noontime meal at the hotel dining room. They had steak and all the trimmings.

"It's a start toward honest self rule," Spur said.

"Damn well about time," Doc said. "We've got notices up for the election. Dug up the laws on it, and who we need to elect. I'll be going to Springfield next week for some advice from the county people there."

Spur cut off a slab of the medium rare steak and worked on it for a minute. "Good steak," he said. He gave Doc Gibson a scrap of paper with his St. Louis office address. "You have any problems, you write me a letter at this office. Word will get to me wherever I am."

"Don't expect any more trouble," Doc said. "But we'll have to see." He paused for a while. "I got one worry, that's Stone county next door. They have a bunch of Bald Knobbers over there, too. Don't know how much they talked to this batch."

"Stand tough, Doc," Spur said. "Stand tough."

After his dinner, Spur stopped by at the Branson general store for some supplies for the trail, then rode toward the cave. As he had done every other time, he watched his back trail, did a quarter mile backtrack, and made sure nobody followed him. He wanted no surprises between now and tomorrow morning.

# 17

When Spur rode into the small clearing near the hidden mouth of the cave, he found Edith sitting in the sun on one of her blankets. She had washed her hair and let it dry in the sun and had combed it out into a black halo.

Spur swung down, unsaddled his horse and set it to grazing on a long tether and put the sack of provisions by the tree. Neither of them had spoken.

He sat down beside her. She made room so he could sit on the blanket close to her.

"Tell me what happened," she said.

He told her, quickly, in detail. "As far as I can tell that band of Bald Knobbers is finished. Fourteen of the twenty core members are dead. As far as we know the rest of them have left town quickly for other parts."

"All of this and you never violated your oath as a lawman, I'm proud of you."

"It worked out. Someday there may come a time when it won't."

"What will you do then?"

"Depends. I'll weigh the benefits against the

personal loss, and if the benefits are great enough to enough people, I'll probably do it."

"Honest, you're so damn honest. I've never known anyone like you before."

"Why aren't you married? You're beautiful, smart, educated, have a good job. Why hasn't some smart man married you?"

"One did. He was killed by a white man in a fight three weeks after we were married."

"Oh, God, no!"

"Yes. It's one of the backlashes from the war. I was waiting for my husband to come, and . . . and this man walked up to me and backed me against a wall. Then he began touching my breasts."

"The bastard!"

"Will came up and saw him and I pushed the man away, but Will wouldn't let it be. He yelled at the man, and ran at him and hit him in the face. The man was a Southerner and before Will could move, the white man drove a knife into my Will and he died in my arms."

"The bastard! How long ago?"

"Two years." She took a long breath and brushed her hand across her eyes. "I kept Will's name." She looked up at Spur. "You remind me a lot of him. About the same size. Strong. A square cut face, and you get things done. Will wanted to be a policeman. He was going to school." She stopped and looked away.

Slowly she moved until she leaned against Spur. She caught his hands and put his arms around her.

"Just hold me tight a minute, it helps."

They sat that way a while, then she moved and he let go of her and she edged away.

"We're heading out in the morning?"

"Yes. Early start and we'll be in Springfield the second day sometime."

"Good. I've had about enough camping out." She stood and stretched, caught his hand and pulled him up. "Help me get us some supper. We can heat up some beans. Did you bring anything from town to eat?"

She looked in the sack and yelped in surprise. There was bacon, eggs, canned peaches, a sack of fresh cherries and two big apples.

"We'll have a feast!" She frowned. "I wonder if that woman and her two children ever made it to Springfield?"

Spur told her about the three bodies that were brought into town.

"Mrs. Newcomb could have killed them. She must have been angry and frightened enough. It doesn't take a good shot to use a shotgun effectively."

"I hope she did, and I hope that she is safe."

"We'll ask when we get there."

An hour later they relaxed after a full supper. Spur cleaned up everything, built up the fire and brought in the blankets from outside where she had aired them.

She spread them out near the fire and sat down. Edith patted the spot beside her and Spur sat there. She reached over and held his face and kissed his lips gently.

"Spur, I've never slept with many men. But I do want to make love with you. It seems so right, so natural. It . . . it's not just gratitude for your saving me twice from that mob. I want to be sure you understand that."

"Yes, Edith, I understand." He reached over and kissed her lips. She responded for a moment, then pushed him back.

"I want to say this. I'm serious. I teach children. I know I have to be a little stronger, a little cleaner, a little better dressed and more careful than other people. These students look up to their teachers. We're models for them.

"So, in Philadelphia I am pure and pristine. But right now I feel like I want you a dozen times. Does that makes sense? I want you on me and in me and loving me every way possible. Even though I know when we get to Springfield I won't even get to ride on the same passenger car as you do. I'll be on the one marked 'Colored Only.' But I don't care. Why is this, Spur McCoy?"

"I don't know, Edith. It has something to do with the perpetuation of the species, I'm sure. But it also has a lot to do with how two people feel about each other. There has to be respect and honesty, and love, even if for just the moment, there always has to be love."

She kissed him and pushed him down gently on the blanket.

"Spur, take off my blouse, please."

He did. She wore nothing under it. Her hanging breasts dangled toward him and he caught one in each hand.

"So good! That feels so good!" She nestled on top of him then, crushing her breasts against his chest, her lips reaching for his.

A minute later she sat up.

"I want to undress you. To do it slowly, to tease you. Can I do that?"

He bent and kissed her breasts and smiled. "Of course, Edith. You can do anything you want to, here with me and back in Philadelphia. Remember that."

She undressed him with loving gentleness.

When they were both naked, she lay across him and stared at the contrasting skin in the firelight.

"Look! So dark, so black, and so white, pink, tanned brown, really. Such a difference!"

"Not so much difference. We both have two legs, two arms, two eyes, one heart, one mind. If we are hurt we cry, if we cut our skin, we bleed. We live, we die. Not so much difference."

"The Knobbers thought so. To them I was an animal."

"The Knobbers were criminals, they were Southern criminals."

She kissed him and smiled. "You're right, not so much difference." She pulled him over on top of her.

"Soft, and easy and slow. Can you make it last a long, long time, Spur not-much-difference McCoy?"

"An hour?"

"I'd die!" she said giggling like a school girl.

She parted her legs and lifted her knees. Spur kissed her and probed gently, found the opening and worked in slowly. At last they were locked together.

"Oh, yes!" She kissed his nose. "Don't move for a minute, or two." She sighed. "Heaven. Now I'll know what to expect when I get there." She moved gently under him, then kissed his chest.

"Tell me about Spur McCoy. We have a whole hour." She gripped him with her internal muscles and Spur yelped. "Just want to be sure you don't go to sleep on me."

He told her about his youth, his life, his fighting in the war.

"Did you kill men, in the war?"

"Yes, from far away with a rifle, in one hand to hand battle with a rebel major when we overran their position. I had to use a knife before he could bring up his pistol."

She shuddered.

He moved gently inside her and she smiled, the terror forgotten.

"Do that again," she said, kissing him hard. Then she climaxed gently and opened her eyes watching him. "I don't want to get you over excited. One time for you, six or seven for me." She kissed him again. "This night, this whole trip, is going to be something I'll remember for the rest of my life."

"Tell me about Edith Washington."

"Not much to tell. I was born in Philadelphia, went to school there, went to two years of special Normal School to get my teaching credentials. Now I teach."

"Brothers, sisters?"

"Two of each." She was silent a minute. "Spur, I'm being unfair. I'm using you shamelessly. I didn't even ask."

"What do you mean?"

"After, after what those men did to me in the street . . . I needed another experience, something to take the bitter taste from my mouth. I might have hated all men forever after that. It was so . . . so brutal . . . like I was a dog in heat. So . . . so . . ." He touched her lips.

"I understand. I'm glad to be able to help. I'm ashamed of those men."

She began moving her hips under him. She grinned at him.

"Good. Now, Spur, let's see how fast you can get where you're going. You've held back long enough." She pushed upward with her hips, lifting him a foot off the ground, then dropped down and he laughed and felt her muscles gripping him and releasing, and within a minute he was counting the stars as he sailed past them on his way to the moon.

They lay locked together for a long time. Then they got up and built the fire, found the cinnamon rolls Spur had hidden from her and ate and drank cold water from the stream.

They made love again, and ate again, and then lost track of the time and the night and when they woke the next time, a sliver of sunshine streamed in the top of the cave.

Gently he kissed her good morning, then they got up and had coffee and packed for the trail.

Outside, Edith stood in her borrowed clothes and looked around.

"I really hate to leave," she said. "So much has happened to me here. I'll never, never forget Branson, Missouri." She looked up at Spur. "And even if I have a dozen reincarnations, I'll never in a million years forget last night."

"You might," Spur said.

"How could I? It was romantic, and honest, and I think I learned something about human nature. How could I ever forget that?"

"About ten miles down is a good sized stream. By the time we get there it will be getting hot and we could decide to take a swim and then warm up on the grass and we might even feel like getting romantic again. Have you ever made love in the water?"

Edith looked at him a minute in surprise, then they both burst out laughing, mounted up and rode down the trail toward Springfield.

[AUTHOR'S NOTE: The historic town of Branson, Missouri exists today. Stone County and Taney County are still there. Both counties were literally independent kingdoms following the Civil War. For twenty years after the war clenched fists and six-guns were the only law there.

The Bald Knobbers controlled Taney and Stone Counties as tightly as the Mafia ran Chicago in the 1920's.

Extortion was their main purpose. If you didn't pay the price, you might be visited on late night raids by horsemen. Beatings and hangings were common. The only law was the law of the Bald Knobbers.

These vigilante groups gone bad were not routed out of power until a pitched battle took place with the Missouri militia which was called out in the late 1880's to settle things once and for all.

Dr. Gibson's new honest government lasted in Branson for almost five years, then the Bald Knobbers from neighboring Stone county moved in and took over until the militia arrived.]